A BOY'S ADVENTURES FROM THE MISSISSIPPI COTTON FIELDS

BY DR. OSCAR MCKINLEY

DORRANCE PUBLISHING CO
EST. 1920
PITTSBURGH, PENNSYLVANIA 15238

Dorrance Publishing Co
585 Alpha Drive
Pittsburgh, PA 15238
Visit our website at *www.dorrancebookstore.com*

ISBN: 979-8-89341-387-8
eISBN: 979-8-89341-885-9

A BOY'S ADVENTURES FROM THE MISSISSIPPI COTTON FIELDS

Dr. Oscar McKinley grew up in Mississippi during the Jim Crow era. In first grade, he began giving away his lunch money to feed hungry kids, and he has devoted his life to helping others ever since. He earned a double doctorate in special education and psychology and also has a degree in religion.

TABLE OF CONTENTS

THE INTRODUCTION

Mary was my mother and she was a very quiet and reserved woman. She was a well-liked within the community. She had respect for herself as well as others, and was aware of how eloquent and beautiful she looked. She expressed her exquisite beauty on many occasions trying to make dad jealous. But it never worked, because dad was too cool. Her weight was less than ninety pounds. She could wear kid's shoes and some of their clothes. I remember on occasions she was mistaken for being a kid. But it didn't bother her at all. She took it a badge of honor. She kept right on smiling and so did my dad. They were a beautiful couple. I never seen them argue. Mom had a positive outlook on life. She had a good sense of humor and could sang like Aretha Franklin. She had confidence and if she made a mistake, she never tried to cover it up. She was a firm believer in accountability. She encourages all her children to be creative and to have a strong work ethic, and be willing to accept change. She was authentic and lead with integrity and honesty.

William, my father, was a man of integrity. He always dressed nice and carried himself as a gentleman. Most of the black people thought he was a white man, because he looked exactly as a white man. Even though he claimed to be black. He looked whiter than most white people. No one could tell he wasn't white. He had the best of both worlds anytime he desired. He always kept a smile on his face and was always nice to the people. No black person knew exactly where he came from. So, there wasn't any way to prove his race. He was a very quiet man, who smiled a lot and never lacked confidence. He was better educated than of my teachers at school. He knew astrology well and taught us about the galaxy. But he was always busy working or helping out other people. He would never argue with anyone, nor use profanity. He was well respected among black people as well as the whites. He also never disrespected women. He was a very nice man. Even though most people considered him to be a very dangerous man. He carried himself well. He gave my brother and I our own personal Winchesters rifles at the age of eleven and twelve and taught us how to shoot. He also taught us how to survive off the land. He was a very handsome man, tall with long Curley hair, and had a walk that made women stop and stare. All races of women went for him. He would give off a smile when women flirted with him. But he was faithful to my mother. I use to love going places with dad, just to watch the women reactions in his presence. He also could play a guitar and sang like Johnny Cash "The Man in Black". Dad always said that Johnny Cash sang like black folks. My dad was a star and I will always love him.

One day we counted all of his firearms and they added up to fifty weapons. He even had a gun hidden in the chicken house, and there wasn't a time that he wasn't carrying a weapon. He was a gun collector. He even took his favorite pistol to bed with him at night, and kept it under his pillar. He protected us from whites as well as blacks. They all feared him. He almost never got angry. But when he did something bad usually happened. He could hurt any black person he wanted, and nothing would happen to him. Just like any other white man could do. White people treated him as a white man. Yet he claimed to be a black man. I often heard people say that my dad was a killer and had shot and killed several people in the past. I didn't believe any of it, and never spoke to my dad about the rumors. But I did notice, whenever he became angry with someone, he would always put his hands on his gun, which he always kept in his back pocket in a paper bag. My dad spoke softly and never raised his voice, but, if he told you something, you best believe him.

Betty, my oldest sister, was around sixteen years of age during this time. She always had a thing for sneaking around kissing older guys. Getting the guys ready then she would run away and laugh. She didn't understand how to cope with the intense feelings of growing into an adult. Instead, she play these games to be in control of the situation. This behavior may have come from something that happen to her at a very young age in childhood. For some strange reason she liked for guys to chase her. While she pretended to not like them. Yet she was constantly teasing them and playing hard to get. She had a grown woman's body and knew what guys wanted. My youngest sister was a different story all together. It was like she wished she was a boy. She could beat me shooting marbles, climbing trees and could almost run as fast as I could. She was the epitome of a tomboy. Anytime we were shorthanded of a football player she would always fill the position, and she could play better than a lot of the guys. She didn't drop passes or miss a tackle. She would tell guys if you get the ball, I'm going to hit you so hard you're going to lose the ball, and she meant business. They were scared of her, because she played angry all the time. I always kept her on my team to feel safe. She had a thing for following me around and starting fights with boys. I see her get in many fights with boys, but only a few with girls. She only wore boys' clothes, unless she was going to school or church. A tomboy at heart and loved wearing cowboy boots and hats, along with tight jeans.

My older brother was a quiet and well-mannered boy who had a special love for money. It appeared that his brain was wired to make money. He always seems happy whenever he got his allowance. He was a proud individual who loved his independence. He would always explain to me the power of money. But it never resonated with me. He never spent his money. He would save every penny and on occasions show me all his money. I would often ask him why are you showing me your money. His answer was always the same. So, you can wish you had money like me. He was around eleven years of age, and could keep his allowance all year without spending a cent. He had a good understanding about life and was able to comprehend most things. I learned a lot from my brother. He was smart in school and never got into any trouble. He could wear a white shirt all day and never get a spot on it. He was like the perfect child. I always wanted to be like him, except I was the direct opposite. He possess all the qualities that makes a boy perfect. He could follow rules to a T. I admired his Integrity and honesty. I can remember setting looking at him and wishing I could be like him. He really influences me to strive for goodness. There was no one else that I witness at the time who had more kindness and goodness as a person. I loved him for being a perfect example. It's was just a win-win situation for everybody who came into contact with him.

Now, it's down to me. I was around ten years old at the time and had a wild streak. But I always felt positive about good attributes in people. I love to see people happy and always went out of my way to accommodate them. If they were nice people, I would always give chance after chance. I wasn't a toxic child, but I didn't follow rules at school. I was terrible with that ordeal. I just didn't like school. I was full of love and kindness. I got into one fight after another. I would often hear kids saying things like, you act like a white boy that I see on television. I hated hearing that quote. It always led to a fight. The thing about me was that I wasn't afraid to get whipped in a fight. Every time I got into a fight; it was like David facing Goliath. I never fought anyone my size because they all were afraid of me.

Therefore, I lost some fights to older guys, but never was I afraid. I didn't feel too bad about fighting, because I always told my mother and repented, because it made me feel good about myself. In fact, there were times I would confess to my parents the wrong that I had done. Knowing the consequences. I hated feeling guilty after doing something wrong. My parents taught us to never lie because lying was a terrible thing to do, and People that did lie were considered diabolically evil doers. Also, people who entice people to lie are demonically insidious and workers against God. I grew up in a good religious home in Mississippi. It was a golden rule in our home to never lie. I could have gotten out of many whippings, if I had only lied. I can remember making the decision to tell the truth like it was yesterday. Let me tell you about some of the times I was tested. I came face to face with it many times.

When I was about eight or nine years old, I started chewing gum at church because I had seen older kids doing it. But I always got caught time and time again. Ushers would come up to me and ask the question, boy, are you chewing gum in church. I would always answer truthfully,

YES. Even though I knew the consequences and I knew they would tell my mother or grandma. I always hoped they would tell Grandma, because her discipline was fast as lightning. She was sort of scary coming up to you breathing loud and looking like the main scene in a scary movie.

Actually, I should have been scared straight. But I would always hold my ground and stand there like a little man and own up to it. POW, right upside the head she went. I really wanted to say afterwards, it was nice doing business with you grandma, it's over. One of the things that I have learned from that philosophy throughout the years is that the truth will always set you free, because it doesn't come back to haunt you.

THE COTTON FIELDS OF MISSISSIPPI
PART ONE:

Me and three of my peers would sneak out the house every Saturday night during the warm months and go running through the cotton fields of Mississippi, usually straight to the country juke house. But not this Saturday night. The moon was full and shining bright, and we headed over to Ms. Lucy's house to see her daughter Bobbie Joe give birth. Our age range was from ten to twelve. Bobbie Joe was one of our playmates and she was ten years old giving birth, and had the appearance of a younger girl. She was very cute with long brown hair with beautiful green eyes. She had light skin and so did I. We got picked on at times because of our light skinned complexion. However, it only made us grow closer. Bobbie Joe had moved into the area about a year earlier. She was the prettiest girl I had ever seen. Her entire head was covered with brown hair, at times it looked to be red. I liked her right away. But I was petrified of ever talking to her. Yet, I was loud but shy, which I thought was a strange combination. Right from the beginning she started telling people that she liked me. So, I was happy to accommodate her. Kids were always under the Impression that we were boyfriend and girlfriend. At least she proclaimed to be my girl. However, I would never own up to being her boyfriend. But I was in love with Bobbie Joe. Even though we were young, our love was strong. Bobbie Joe was mature for her age and always wanted to show affection. I went along as far as I could, but she always wanted more. My mother explained to me about girls being able to get pregnant at her age. It scared me.

So, every time Bobby Joe seemed to want to experience other things. I always ran home. I felt sorry for Bobbie Joe being pregnant at ten years old. I felt like it was my fault. She had just written me a three-page love letter, just two days earlier, while being nine months pregnant, expressing her love for me. The letter made me feel like a small man at the age of ten. She assured me that I was the only man in her life. She had a way with words. She even talked about how good I made her feel. She made me think twice about being the true father. I know I use to kiss her a lot. But now I was beginning to think kissing was having sex. Bobby Joe kept saying in her letter that I was the father. Well, Bobbie Joe was so beautiful and nice to me; I didn't know how to say no to her. I remember the day I met her. The dialogue went sort of like this.

We both were nine years old. It went sort of like this:

Bobbie Joe: Why are you so violent?
Answer: I only fight to protect people that I like.
Bobbie Joe: Looks like you get beat up a lot, they're too big for you to fight
Answer: Yeah, but I always count on my first lick and I always go first, that scars them a little.
Bobbie Joe: You think you bad, don't you?
Answer: No, I go to church.
Bobbie Joe: Do you want to marry me when you grow up?
Answer: I'll fight somebody for you.
Bobbie Joe: Ok then. You can be my boyfriend?
Answer: Sure, but I don't like kissing.
Bobbie Joe: OK, just a kiss on Saturdays and I tongue kiss.
Reply: Your tongue is made for talking. We don't need to do that one.
Bobbie Joe frowns and starts to cry.
Reply: What's wrong?
Bobbie Joe: You don't love me.
Reply: (looks puzzled and rubs his head). I do love you. I said I will fight for you, didn't I? Do you want me to go get into a fight?
Bobbie Joe: Yes.
Reply: OK.
Bobbie Joe: No, please don't fight. I don't want to see you hurt. I love you too much.
Then she hugs and tongue kisses me. Right in front of my friends.

Reply: Aww, that didn't feel right.
Bobbie Joe: We can kiss better than that with practice.
Reply: Are you sure?
Bobbie Joe: Yes, I'm sure.

Well, that's how I met Bobbie Joe. From that day forward we were considered to be dating. Yes, I was in love with her and she was in love with me. She often would tell me how much she loved me and always talked about sex. But I had no idea how to explain sex and wasn't interested. She would talk about watching her mother do it. I didn't really pay much attention to that conversation. I never thought she wanted to experience it so bad until she would have sex with someone else. But Bobbie Joe wanted to know and I was scared to try. I felt like I had failed her.

I remember one day asking her why she liked me. Her answer was quick and direct. She stated I was the only person she knew, who wasn't afraid of anything, except sex. I wanted so badly to tell her that I had given my mother my word that I wouldn't have sex with her. Then she explained that she felt safe around me. Well, that wasn't anything new, because I had heard that kind of talk lots of times from friends, who were mostly older. I was young, but I acted like a little man.

Well, the summer was almost over and it was a Saturday night deep in the Mississippi Delta. A night to remember.

When we arrived at Bobbie Joe's, there was a crowd of people gathered around Ms. Lucy's house, waiting for Bobbie Joe to give birth. There stood this little cute shack about three miles from the edge of the woods, that was surrounded by cotton as far as one could see. The people were gathering and having fun, some were drinking alcohol and playing a portable record player. It was sort of like a juke house. People were dancing and gambling. They even had two ladies frying and selling fish sandwiches. It felt like a real juke house. The stars filled the sky shining bright that night, and in some strange way I felt like I was becoming a father. I had heard older people talking about when a woman is giving birth the father feels the pain as well. I believe there's something to that, because it hurt me really bad, down in my stomach, every time Bobbie Joe screamed. Even though I knew nothing about having sex. I still felt responsible for Bobbie Joe. The house was filled with people who lived on the Swan plantation. They were all waiting on the arrival of my so-called secret son. The house had four-rooms with large fans in all the windows. All the doors were wide open except Bobbie Joe's room. Mosquitos were flying all over the house biting people. After a while people started hitting each other trying to kill the misquotes. Several fights broke out. While Bobbie Joe was screaming to the top of her lungs trying to deliver our baby.

Her mother Ms. Lucy was screaming almost as loud as Bobbie Joe on the back porch having sex with most of the men. Robert, who was one of my friends, was among the men and he was twelve-year-old. He wanted to have sex with Ms. Lucy as well. But she kept saying no, he's too young. The men waiting in line explained that he was waiting just as they were and that she shouldn't keep holding up the line. So, she went on and had sex with Robert. He was young, strong, and really big for his age. He got Mrs. Lucy going. She started screaming loud and louder and making more noise than Bobbie Joe giving birth. Mrs. Lucy was a very quiet woman who had exquisite beauty. She could get any man's attention. She really looked like a beauty queen, when she fixed herself up.

Men were always fighting over her. She had a perfect figure (Coca-Cola bottle) and was always ready to put out for men, sadly to say.

The reason for Ms. Lucy sexual promiscuity behavior started right after her son was lynched. She lost her son to a lynching five years back, simply because her son opened the car door for a white girl. So, ever since then, Mrs. Lucy used sex to provide a position of contentment, and well-being. Everyone within the house started asking if there was somebody else having a baby out back. Her husband recognized Mrs. Lucy's loud moaning and went out back and caught her having sex with Robert. He Immediately got into a fist fight with twelve-year-old Robert. Mrs. Lucy started breaking up the fight between Robert and her husband saying "stop fighting over me". That part made all of my friends laugh.

We witnessed our friend in a fight over a grown woman. Her statement got the attention of other adults, including Robert's mother. After finding out what had taken place the boy's mother ran out back and began fighting Mrs. Lucy. They took the fight inside and broke down the bedroom door and got on the bed fighting while Bobbie Joe was still giving Birth. I went into the bedroom trying to help break up the fight. Because I didn't want to see Bobbie

Joe hurt. Plus, I was trying to protect my so-called son. However, through it all Bobbie Joe gave birth to a six-pound baby boy. After the delivery the fighting and partying stopped. All of a sudden it became quiet and everyone started heading home, and that included us.

THE JUKE HOUSE

But we decided to swing by the juke house before going home. It was sitting right on the edge of a fishing pond. Upon arrival we noticed two of the cars parked outside were rocking back and forth. We looked through the window of the cars and saw a married woman in each of the cars with men whom we recognized as being married as well, but to another woman.

We Immediately made a promise to each other not to tell on the married women committing adultery. Inside the juke house smelled like a load of funk. It seemed that the people there were contributing the funkiest load of funk ever. I believed it was enough funk to last a thousand years, and most of them were doing a dance called the funky Broadway. It couldn't have been funkier. We went inside and stayed as long as we could. It was so exciting getting to see the country celebrity dancers. I loved every minute of it.

There was always a dance going on at the country juke house and sometimes they had blues bands playing there, and these were famous people. Plus, there was nearly always someone there from Chicago or Detroit doing the latest dances. It was one of the best Juke houses around. I think because of the richness of the land that made cotton plentiful. Most people had money, but not a lot, because it didn't take much money to have a good time in those days. The country dancers didn't need a partner. They went at it alone. All they needed was the right music and they all took to the floor, and boy did they mean business. Some still had on their dirty work clothes, and funk was flying all over the place, but they kept getting down on it. They came to party and it was obvious that they didn't care what someone thought of them. It was fun watching but scary at the same time, because if anyone by mistake ran into another dancer anything could jump off and here's the kicker, the women were more dangerous than the men. I think the most dangerous couple was a skinny tall lady with a short dumpty fat husband. When she got to going and partying hard, she always took out her pistol and waved it around in the air. While her fat short husband took out his ice pick in one hand, while holding her purse on his arm just as a woman. The other most dangerous couple was a short stocky woman who had the appearance of a man. She would carry a sawed-off shotgun under her dress and her husband carried a short ax in his overhauls. There were many more dangerous people in the juke. But these couples were notorious. Actually, it was frightening being around such dangerous people. They also had a gambling room. The gambling room always attracted our attention for a while, because we wanted to see who was winning. It always gave me an advantage over the winner. Because usually I knew who his wife was along with his girlfriend.

It was a well-kept secret about who the winner was from the dice game. Because there were a lot, Beggars. One man always had crooked dice and cheated. He was not allowed to participate in the game and it was house rules. However, he would always enter his girlfriend in the game and very few people knew that they were dating. But I knew some of their deepest secrets. Along with most of the people at the Juke house. So, they always bough me what ever I wanted and treated me like a king. My friends could never figure out why. They often asked me, but I never told.

So, after a while at the juke house some of us became sleepy and soon we found ourselves headed back home through the cotton fields of Mississippi. We snuck back into our windows and went to bed as though nothing had happened.

SPY 007

I didn't see Bobbie Joe back in the cotton fields after giving birth for three weeks. So, I rode around every day on the mule and I always knew who was picking cotton that particular day from who wasn't. I used to hang out with the mule boy in the cotton field. The task of the mule boy was to haul the cotton sacks to the trailer to be weighted and stored. He was also the messenger boy. Because in the cotton fields people would be too far apart to communicate with each other. Plus, the cotton stalks were usually too tall to locate them. So, here is where the mule boy came into the picture. He would stand up on the mule and locate the person and go deliver the message. It was considered the best type of communication during that time. Equivalent to today's cell phone.

On many occasions the mule boy didn't like delivering messages, so he would send me and that happened almost 99% of the time. That made me a very Important person in the cotton fields. Because I knew everybody's business, they trusted me with their life. On many occasions they would send a message to their lovers and most of the people were married.

Well, this is how I became so popular in the cotton fields of Mississippi. I was 007 at the age of ten. I was the man. People would try to bribe me all the time for information, along with trying to con me out of a bottle of my uncle's corn whiskey. It was my job selling corn whiskey in the cotton field. But I never gave anyone whiskey without pay, because I would never double cross my uncle. He was a hardnosed Mississippi gangster, who didn't take kindly to being double crossed. So, the people trusted me because I could keep my mouth shut, plus I always took care of my business. No information got out and the people loved me for doing it. I had lots of practice because my uncle taught me all about his business. He trusted me to know where everything was kept, even how to make it.

I never told my parents about the secrets that I kept with my uncles. I had one that lived in Mississippi and another that lived in Chicago. They were both serious notorious gangsters and they trusted me with their lives. So, I knew the seriousness of keeping my mouth shut. I didn't even tell my friends about the dangerous things they had me involved with. Even till this day, I haven't told the secrets of the Mississippi cotton fields, until now. Maybe one day I will share more of its secrets.

Anyway, this particular day the message was to Ms. Lucy and Bobbie Joe. At first, I didn't want to go, because Bobbie Joe had been hiding from me. She was ashamed of being a mother at ten years old. But I didn't think much of it. Anyway, the message was to come home because the baby is sick.

So, I put Bobbie Joe on the back of the mule behind me and gave her a ride home. She held on so tight, all the while crying. The way she held me in her arms that day has never been matched. Bobbie Joe had the magic touch. I really loved that beautiful country girl and I'm sure she loved me. She kept saying over and over again how much she loved me. I don't think I said a mumbling word. But she made me make a promise that day that we would always be together. I nodded my head as though I agreed with her. I couldn't speak.

To this very day I don't know who Bobby Joe's baby father was, except he was an older man. Ms. Lucy always had men hanging around her house. Bobby Joe use to tell me about men coming in her room at night. But I paid it no mind. I never would have suspected a grown man of having sex with Bobby Joe.

THE OLD MAN

There was always entertainment going on in the cotton fields of Mississippi. One in particular that stood out from the rest was this old man. I can remember this old man as though it was yesterday. He wore knee pads and would pick cotton so slowly and fall so far behind until I would ride the mule back several times a day to check on him.

As soon as the white bossman came to the cotton field in the afternoon. The old man would get right in front of the white man. Every time he turned; he would get right in front of him again. If the bossman didn't give him enough attention he would pass out. It always scared all the women and sometimes the bossman. He was well liked and no one knew his exact age. Some of the people said that he was in his eighties and some said nineties.

But every evening when the bossman arrived, all the women would pressure the bossman to show him plenty of attention. Because when he passed out sometimes it took an hour or so before he would come out of it. No one wanted that. They all wanted to go home including the bossman. So, he would assist the old man on many occasions and go along with the gag. The old man would roll his eyes back in his head. Take off his shirt and start making faces over and over again. He would act as though he had worked so hard until he couldn't take another step. Like it was back breaking work. Most of the time the women would give him cotton. He couldn't pick no more than 50 pounds of cotton.

The funny thing about that show was he was acting. The boss man would be acting weird alongside the old man. The bossman would start saying things to the old man as though they were feeding off each other. Dam, you have done so much work today. Here's a quarter stop by the store and get you a cold soda and cool down. You're working too hard. Make sure you get some rest tonight. Then he would follow the old man around. He would be frowning and dancing around saying things like I have the best worker in the world right here in this cotton field. Everybody started clapping. He would be making faces and looking right at the old man. They sometimes fell on the ground together and started rolling around in the dirt. They would put on the show at least twice a week at quitting time. It was so funny.

The same bossman used to always play around with me. Saying things like, would you like to own this mule. I would always say yes, and his reply was maybe next time, I'll give him to you. I always laugh and that seemed to make him happy. He really liked my dad and he used to always single me out. I liked him because he was funny. He liked me because I wasn't afraid of him. I know because he told me one day. It sorts of went like this. He said Oscar, you have more nerves than I do. My reply was yes.

CHICAGO

Three months after birth Ms. Lucy and Bobbie Joe moved to Chicago Illinois. It took me six years to see her again. I usually traveled to Chicago at least two to three times a year. But never knew where she lived. One day my brother-in-law asked me if I wanted to see her again. He had visited Ms. Lucy a week before and knew where they lived. He explains that she was inquiring about me. Immediately, I said yes. I was sweet sixteen and she was still the love of my life. So, off we went. She lived on the East side of Chicago. I wasn't familiar with that area. Most of my relatives lived on the south side. During that time gangs played a big part in where a young black male went. I was sort of into The Disciples gang, because I was in their territory. But I never really committed to any gang.

Well, upon arrival on the East side of Chicago. Her block was filled with Black Stone Rangers. A gang that most gangs feared, including the police. But I didn't think much of it. I was going to see my wife. She had informed one of the gang members that her son's father was on his way over to see his son. So, one of the guys took it upon himself to try to scare me away. He and about ten other gang members were there waiting on me. Yes, but we had brought along a little company as well. But I wanted to make sure I got a chance to see Bobbie Joe before the trouble started. So, I asked everyone to stay in the car. I got out alone and walked past the guys. Nothing was said, and no eye contact. Bobbie Joe ran out of the house crying and hugged me. She showed me my so-called son. A little boy who resembled me, to the T. His very first words to me were hi daddy, I love you. I picked him up and gave him a big kiss and hug, then I began to cry with Bobbie Joe. I couldn't hold back the tears. I held both of them in my arms. It truly was one of the best feelings of my entire life. I was surprised to find out that Bobbie Joe was telling people that I was the father. That was not a problem, because I had already decided that I was the father, when I was ten years old. Well, there she was right in front of me again. Looking so beautiful. I was sure that she was the prettiest woman in the whole wide world, and she was still in love with me. I walked in that house that day and ended up staying six months. I quit school in Mississippi that year.

However, it was an everyday challenge, living on the east side of Chicago. I get into fights at least three times a week. But it never deterred me to leave Bobby Joe. I felt like my dream had come true and I wasn't going to leave Bobbie Joe. Afterall, if there was ever anyone tough enough to fight back each time, it would have to have been me. I was betting on myself to be the toughest. YEAH. I got into somewhere around thirty fights. Death threats were made on continual basics and I got shot at three times. But, after a while, they finally respected me and left me alone. Most of the guys that I fought started bragging to me and became true friends.

Finally, I had my woman to myself for the second time in my life and it felt good. We used to take long walks along the beach right off Lake Shore Drive holding hands. All the guys were watching her and most of the girls were watching me, and we were keeping an eye on each other. We were so close; I could hear her heartbeat. She was so sexy. I can remember her asking me to do certain things for her and I would say no sometimes. She would then look deep into my eyes. It sometimes frightens me, because her eyes always started changing colors, plus she had a look that penetrated your soul. Soon it became a struggle for me to say no to her. I can honestly say that she was the most beautiful woman in the entire world. We were inseparable at the time. Well, after about four months, I felt it was time to visit my Chicago uncle again.

He was a hustler who dabbled in many things, to make money. His main business was selling corn whiskey that we sent him from Mississippi.

I can remember him taking me to a place called "The Hold in the Wall" in Chicago on the west side, which had a gambling room, food for sale and prostitutes running around. They didn't want to let me in, because they stated that I was too young. My uncle knew that they were greedy for money, so he told them about my skills. He stated, this is the boy from Mississippi that I was telling you about. He knows how to make corn whiskey. My uncle knew that I would never tell how it was done. After that day, I was always welcome there, anytime I wanted to stop by. Some guys had brand new Cadillacs and others had fine rides, and they always offered me a ride whenever I was leaving. Sometimes I rode along.

It wasn't long before I started selling corn whiskey for my uncle in Chicago. It gave me power over a lot of street thugs. It also helps me keep a pocket of money. At the time I loved to dress like a street hustler. Pimps would always come up to me asking about my outfits. But I knew most of them would never dress like me. Because I was on the low, not too fly. I had several leather boots that had different colors and the leather jackets matched, along with my caps, and they were all tailor made. My dressing was so cold until people would stop and stare, as I passed. My uncle also took me to places on Cottage Grove and Madison Street in Chicago to other places, that I would consider a hole in the wall. They all called my uncle by his street name. I was happy to go along, because it was good for business. I was only sixteen years old and my uncle had turned the corn whiskey game over to me in the streets of Chicago. He had other ways of making money and it kept him busy. So, it wasn't a problem for me to run the business, because I had another uncle in Mississippi who let me run the business and had trained me well. So, I knew the game at the time, and I truly felt that I was at the top of my game. I was a serious matter to deal with. To me the streets of Chicago was like being in a candy store, and I could eat all the candy I wanted. The pimps even gave me a street name. I was called Little Cotton King and I loved it. They were well-known pimps that named me.

Chicago streets were treacherous and cut throat, but I had seen it all in Mississippi. So, I could handle it with ease. Some people say at times I had the coldest look that they had ever seen. So cold until it frightens a lot of street people. Yeah, I was young, but I mean business, and no one was taking over my uncle's business, why I was in charge. I made it known that dangerous people didn't faze me. To me they were the same people I had left behind in Mississippi that I knew so well growing up. I understood how to communicate with dangerous people. The best thing to do is to give them respect and above all stay out of their business. But for me the number one thing was to not see nor hear anything that went on, or was going on. I was the master at keeping my mouth shut. Yeah, it made Chicagoans love me as well as the Mississippi people in the cotton field. The people who knew me trusted me.

But I still ran into problems with certain people known as pimps. I never got along with the pimps, because I felt they were disrespectful. They never seemed to be cool, and respect my game. They were a lot older than I, but they never seem to learned to stop sending their ladies after me. It was a nightmare dealing with them. Because my game was too smooth for that kind of action. Plus, everything they were doing was out in the open. They were like little kids to me. I didn't like their life style, because I worked secretly. I had no interest in pimps, neither becoming one. Even though I always got offers to join the business, and the offers started at a young age.

Now later in life there were times I was tempted to pimp, but all I seen was a bunch of uneducated women with little hungry kids at home that were out of school. I hated it. I couldn't pimp, because I always felt sorry for the women. I actually got into several fights with a couple of pimps, because their lady ran to me. It angered my uncle who was a very powerful man in certain parts of Chicago. So, that was the end of the disrespect coming from the pimps. I had more muscle on the streets of Chicago in certain areas, than most of them. So, I demanded respect. But here's what got me out of the game. It was something unexpected. I was walking down 63rd Street one day and met this lady with her little son. Out of the blue, he started talking to me. He explains that he would never wear my style of clothes. So, out of curiosity I asked him why? He stated because a black man looks better in a dark suit and tie, and at home with his family. That was Strange coming from a little boy. It made me stop in my tracks. Well, I later learned that his father was a Muslim and was teaching his son how to be a man. The same as my father had taught me. A week later I begin to fall apart, because that little boy had planted the seed of success inside me all over again. That's all it took to get my undivided attention, to walk away from the game. Afterwards, all I could hear was Jesus' voice calling me. I started developing a deep hatred for the streets of Chicago. Because I realized I was on a path to destruction.

Yet and still in the fall. I went back to Mississippi and started school again. I left without saying good-bye to Bobbie Joe. I heard she had nerves break down after I left. I felt guilty all over again. I didn't go to Chicago that year for Christmas, nor did I go the next summer. One year later Ms. Lucy moved to California and Bobbie Joe went along. In fact, I have never seen Bobbie Joe again in person, except for her being in movies and on television. She had changed her name and went on to teach at a prestigious University. Oh yeah, If I called her name, a lot of you would recognize it. But that will never happen.

THE CREEPY WALK

After returning from Chicago, I had a girlfriend in high school that lived way out in the country. When I was a teenager, sometimes my car wasn't running, or my ride forgot to pick me up. So, I had to walk home. It was one of the creepiest walks I have ever taken. I had heard about this white man that they called Wild Cat and how dangerous he was. The word was that, he had taken part in almost every lynching that took place within a hundred miles, for the last forty years. He had grown older but every now and then, you would still hear bad things about him. I remember one black man talking about how he kicked two black men that were working for him at the same time. Using both feet, which I thought was funny. He was a dangerous white man. Some people said he was high up the chain of the KKK.

The kicker was that I had to walk Past his house on a dark road deep in the country where no one else was around. I was a very good distance runner, but, as soon as I was near his house. I always stopped running and began to walk very slowly. It was always on a Saturday night, If I had to walk it was usually around the same time when I usually came past his place. He had a bunch of hunting dogs, and they would warn him about fifteen minutes before I arrived. It would be so dark, but he would always be there, standing on the side of the road smoking a cigarette. He stayed on the side of the road by his house and I always kept to the other side. I would stare at him and he would stare at me, but nothing was said. After I was about two hundred yards past his house, I would start running again. This went on for a while until I got my ride fixed. But, one night he said something to me and I stopped walking to hear what he had to say. He asked me if I was afraid of walking the dark roads.

My answer made him laugh. I said, it's okay as long as I don't run into any crazy people.

Right away he knew who I was. He told me to tell my dad hi, and he called him by name. From that night on whenever I came past his house. He always struck up a conversation. Sometimes talking for an hour. He was funny. One day I decided to tell the older man sitting under the shade tree that he was nice to me. None believed me, except my dad. Wild Cat even shared some of his secrets with me. I told him that I only heard bad things about him. He explained that he was rough when he was younger, but he had changed. I don't think he had anyone else to talk to, except me. I felt sorry for him. I believe he would have told me many more of his secrets, If I had asked. But I wouldn't. I considered that crazy old man a friend of mine.

However, my curiosity had got the best of me and I went by his house one Friday afternoon. I wanted to know who lynched Mrs. Lucy's son and I knew he would tell me the truth. He was reluctant to talk about that particular lynching. I could tell it bothered him the most and I could see the pain on his face. I believed he participated in that lynching. After a while of going back and forth. Wild Cat begins to talk about some of the bad things he had done. But he stayed clear of that particular lynching. He stated he wish he could take it all back, and he looked into my eyes, and he appeared so sad. Right then, I wanted to leave, because I could tell, he was about to cry. I couldn't stand to see that. So, I left his house that day carrying his secrets to this very day. I know I could have gotten him to tell me anything I wanted to know about Mrs. Lucky's son's lynching. But I spared him the pain that day. On my way out he asked me again if I will remember him. I assured him that I would. We had become true friends.

I still hold some secrets that he shared, that I will never tell. Because he was my friend. Also, I think he was one of the people protecting me. Because I had gotten into several fights with white boys and nothing was said by any white man, not even a threat. I can remember the last time I talked to him. He asked me a strange question. Would I ever forget him, then he turned and walked away. My answer was no and it seemed to make him happy. I knew right away that something was wrong. That was my last time seeing a wild cat. He passed away one week later. I grieved over the old man, but came to find out my dad was grieving too.

So, we shared many conversations talking about a wild cat. He had told my dad a lot of nice things about me. Dad said that he had a lot of respect for me. As for me to this very day I'm still struggling with my feelings, because I actually admired him. But I was afraid to show it because of all the bad things I heard about him. I asked my dad if it was wrong to feel this way. Dad simply stated, Oscar , you are so different from the rest of us. Please don't deny your feelings, because that's who you are, son.

THE SATURDAY AFTER BOBBIE JOE'S BIRTH

The very next Saturday afternoon, a middle-aged white man approached our house. He had raggedy clothes with holes in his shoes and a hat that looked like it was time to retire. He needed a bath, because he was smelling loud and the smell was fish. I thought maybe he had just caught a fish from the creek about a hundred yards away, and ate it raw. He kept picking his teeth and had a big smile on his face. He seemed to be friendly. He asked for my dad. My mom was afraid of the stranger, so she never responded to the man.

The stranger impacted me in a very different way, because he reminded me of someone I knew, which happened to be my dad. I felt sorry for him and became curious as to why he was there asking about my dad. So, I went and got some of dads' old clothes and a pair of shoes and gave them to the stranger with some soap and a towel. Then I pointed him toward the creek to freshen up. Upon returning the man's appearance featured dad even more. In fact, they looked exactly alike. Most people thought my dad was a white man anyway. Dad could always pass for white, but he always insisted he was a black man. Afterwards, I struck up a conversation. I was curious about his condition, being a white man and all.

My first question to the stranger was did someone rob him of his possessions.

He answered in a very sophisticated way. His words were "I'm sure you have preconceived ideas about me, but I am happy enjoying life, just the way I am". He went on to say that he had plenty of material things in the past. But none of them gave him the peace he needed to evaluate himself and do some critical thinking, which brought internal peace and acceptance. He was then able to judge people on uniqueness instead of their race. I stood there a few seconds struggling with the word preconceived. I had never heard the word before. I tried to look him in the eyes, but his stare at me was piercing cold. He looked at me as though he knew me. I just turned and walked away and stated dad will be home soon. Right then the stranger called me by name and that actually scared me. Immediately he recognized my fear and began to speak.

He explained that dad had written to him at his old address and told him about each one of his kids. So, he assumed my name was Oscar. Since I'm the outspoken one. I assured him that he was correct and that I have always been accused of sometimes talking too much. He smiled and shook my hand then stated that talking sometimes can serve a good purpose. He stated it could be a good thing. Then he gave me some advice, but always remember to listen as well. I nodded my head.

He then smiled and waited to get my reactions before proceeding in a caution manner. I could tell that he was very sensitive to not say anything, or let any of his actions offend me. He looked up at the sky and slowly looked down toward me and gave me another smile. I also did not want to say anything, or give the impression of disrespect. I felt a great similarity for respecting him. It was one of the warmest greetings I have ever felt meeting someone. Then all of a sudden he began to speak about my name. He explained that my name was the most powerful name within the McKinley family. It was as though he worshipped me. But maybe it was my name. I Immediately asked him why. He simply said maybe he'll get a chance to explain later. Although it went over my head, it still had a ring to it that was quite pleasant. He told me many stories about me that dad had shared with him, even the embarrassing ones. He even knew my closest friends' names. He intrigued me. He laughed and stated that I was doing a good job living up to my name. That sounded interesting and I returned a smile. I think it affected him in some type of way, because all of a sudden the stranger sat down and began rubbing his head and looking directly at me. Then He stated that I was exactly like my dad, when he was around my age. He explains that dad loves helping people. This made me more curious about the stranger. How could a white man possibly know about my dad growing up and on top of that he had such a resemblance of dad, as though they were twins.

I knew blacks and whites didn't have much dealing with each other in those days. Something my mom had taught me. But dad never spoke of race.

Not one time except to tell us if we had any trouble with whites to always let him know immediately.

I always thought it was strange. A black man who had no fears of whites. Dad was always a mystery to me. But all my siblings didn't seem to give it a second thought.

It wasn't long, we saw dad coming down the dusty road driving his Chevrolet car. It was a ride that dad took pride in driving. He drove up and parked in the front yard. The minute dad laid eyes on the man he jumped out of his car and ran towards the man and gave him a big hug. They were so glad to see one another. It was obvious they were unequivocally brothers. But, as for me and the family we were left with a disposition overwhelmed with astonishment.

Then we felt distant from Dad and began talking among ourselves. How in the world could a black man and a white man look like twins. That night at the dinner table the stranger told us his name which was James Williams McKinley IV. At that moment we began to look at one another with curiosity, because our last name was McKinley as well. They laughed and talked about their relatives and seemed to be having so much fun. James however had some bad news to tell Dad. He stated that the one white person who was trying to help get their land back had passed away and that the last of their family land had been sold. Dad explains that we were the true bloodline of The Great McKinley Plantation heritage. Simultaneously, both men said the land should be ours and proclaimed to be among the richest people in the world and they were adamant about It. After enjoying his meal James began to speak. He started telling this strange story about a slave master whom he explained was a great, great, great grandfather.

Dad also participated in telling the story by adding bits and pieces of some of the things the stranger overlooked in telling the story. They were family members alright. So, dad was white after all. It was something that me and my mom often discussed, because the two of us were suspicious if dad was a white man. But we could never conclude it as being a true fact, not until now. However, I didn't want to hear my dad admit he was a white man. So, I left the room and started crying. Both men came and brought me back to the table and sat me down. That's when I found that my step dad was actually my real dad. Mom didn't even clear the table because she was embedded in the thoughts of helping me to understand that my dad was a white man. Mom knew all along that he was white. I felt betrayed; however, I loved my dad no matter what race he proclaimed to be. So, we all sat still and listened to a story that memorized our entire household. After I settled down again dad stood up at the table and began to speak. He stated that they both grew up in the same rich household and they were twins. I was always suspicious of dad being a white man, but never suspected him of being rich. They were both extremely handsome men and well educated. The only difference between the two was one considered himself to be a white man and the other a proud black man. Making this story even more interesting.

THE SLAVE MASTER
PART TWO

They told a story about a young slave master named James William McKinley who was only twenty-one years old when he inherited a fortune from his father. Seven years later his wealth had doubled since taking over The McKinley Plantation. He had turned it into the largest plantation in Mississippi with over two thousand slaves. Master McKinley was actually the richest man in America. He owned the largest house by far in all America. Everyone who visited The McKinley Plantation said it was like a palace. It was extremely extravagant with most pieces crafted in Britain and France and shipped straight to Master McKinley's plantation. The house had cedar wood and marble in nearly every place it would fit.

There were more house and yard slaves than any other slave owner in America. It was said that the slaves who worked the yards using their own imagination and creating what they felt the yard should look like. It worked out well for Master McKinley. Because all his guests who toured the yard always said it was the largest and most beautiful flower garden they had ever seen. This always seems to make Master McKinley happy. He would tell his guest how he sent teams to South America in search of finding new flowers to keep up his tradition of having the most exotic and beautiful flower garden the world has ever seen. He also bragged about how most of his house slaves went to Great Britain to learn to serve guests as one would serve a king.

They were professionals and well known as the best servants in America. It was a grand place to set foot inside, especially the ball room. It was built to accommodate three hundred people, and Master McKinley loved everything about it. He enjoyed entertaining the rich. He also had a special likeness for his house and yard slaves because they made him look good, and helped make him plenty of money. He had slave girls who could hold a conversation better than 90% of white women. On many occasions, northerners and foreigners would fall deeply in love with them, and make pleads for their hand in marriage.

They were beautiful sophisticated biracial ladies, who looked as though they could pass for being white. All trained to tease and swindler white men out of their wealth. Master McKinley always dressed his house slaves better than 95% of slave owners' wives. Many slave owners would send their wives along with some of the house slaves to The McKinley Plantation to learn to be graceful, polite, and socially acceptable for ladylikeness. Many of his house slaves also spoke three different languages, which mesmerized men from all over the world. His house slaves were so beautiful and eloquent, and knew that Master McKinley would never part with them. So, they were free to go about the house as pleased.

The McKinley Plantation had thirty-two bed rooms set aside for visitors and he always encouraged his guests to stay for at least one week. But there was one catch: they all had to gamble with cards, or horse races. He also made sure each visitor paid fifty dollars up front in gold, diamonds or silver before they could enter any room.

To make sure he had a steady supply of beautiful girls. Master McKinley would send out teams that travel all over the southern states looking for beautiful young biracial slave girls to buy. He would pay astronomical prices for them. He had teachers on site, but still sent some of the girls off to Britain to learn ladylikeness.

Master McKinley would sometimes exaggerate and say he owned over three thousand slaves. People would believe him, because he was so rich and none of his guests actually got a chance to see his slaves.

Master McKinley knew that field hand slave girls were often raped and subject to all kinds of sexual evil, and malicious wicked acts. A beautiful field hand slave girl had to work all day and still preform at least three to five sexual acts with any white man who cornered her. It was often young white teens.

The overseers along with their sons had their way with any female field hand at any given time. But Master McKinley would kill any white man who disrespected any of his house slaves. He had a special likeness for them. Because they made him look good and above all, made him money. However, the field hands were treated badly and usually kept out of sight from the house and yard slaves. Many house and yard slaves only saw field hands at a distance including Master McKinley.

Master McKinley would never let the house and yard slaves see how the field hands were actually treated. He didn't want them to see the true cruelty of slavery. It was a direct order that Master McKinley enforced even to the death of three white men. So, with that kind of communications some negros on the McKinley plantation had no understanding of the cruelty of slavery.

Master McKinley also wanted no interactions from the overseer with his house and yard slaves. They were his extended family and it was very important to Master McKinley to have happy house and yard slaves. It always seems to please his northern and foreign visitors. Since they were the ones who bet the most money on the horse races. Meaning house slaves and yard slaves never felt the cruel hand of the overseer's whip. Master McKinley even built small brick houses that he kept hidden from his guest behind the tall bushes and flower trees that were for his house and yard slaves to live.

All house slaves could read and write and it was no white man's business. If they tried to interfere with anything Master McKinley did, it usually mean death.

Master McKinley did not believe in just any fight, it had to be to the death. He had bodyguards all over the place, and they were black and white. All the house and yard slaves were treated with dignity and respect. Something which another slave owner hated. But Master McKinley didn't care, not one bit. He was the law in his county and horse races were his main income. In fact, it's how Master McKinley really made his money. Not only had horse racing made him rich, but it also made him one of the most famous men in the world. Everyone with a fast horse in the world wanted to race Master McKinley horses. He owned the most expensive horses in the world and sold them for a good profit. Most people called him the richest man in America. A title which he welcomed and gaveled at the conversation of being the richest man in America.

OSCAR'S BIRTH

This story took wings in the year 1828. A young biracial slave boy named Oscar McKinley was born on a hot September morning. This particular morning had a slight breeze blowing across the hillside and the sun was making its way up. All signs pointed to another hot day in the Mississippi delta. The roosters are crowing loudly. It was going to be another hot day. The sun was considered a killer in Mississippi that summer. Because of the heat it generated, making heat stroke a prevalent thing. It was about 5 am this particular morning. The birth of Oscar took place on Master James William McKinley Plantation deep in the Mississippi Delta. The story tellers stated that Master McKinley had poisoned his father and took over The McKinley Plantation some years earlier. Because his father wanted to sell a certain slave girl named Mattie. A girl who was the apple of Young Master Mckinley's eye. He was madly in love with her. She was the beautiful slave girl whom young Master McKinley couldn't live without.

So, he killed his own father in order to keep Mattie on The McKinley Plantation. Baby Oscar was the son of the plantation owner Master James William McKinley. His mother Mattie was a beautiful fifteen-year-old biracial slave girl who carried herself as if she was the Queen of the Nile. She was the love of Master McKinley's life. He would kill anyone who interfered with his love affair with Mattie. Oscar looked so white at birth, until Master McKinley changed his mind about race with Oscar and completely associated Oscar as being white.

Mattie died from childbirth and Oscar would be his only white son. He didn't have a son and wanted one so badly. So, Oscar became his own white son. Master McKinley put the word out that Oscar's mother came from Britain and gave birth. Afterwards she went back to Britain. Whispers always went on about Oscar's race. There were four house slaves who witnessed the birth and two whites. However, Master McKinley was adamant about Oscar never being called a negro, to the point of committing murder.

Master McKinley killed three of the slaves who witnessed Oscar's birth along with one of the whites. Old Mama Sue who was the negro that raised Master McKinley was spared along with his mother, Bonnie McKinley. But they both knew their life was in danger. Mama Sue was a biracial slave woman around fifty years of age that could pass for being thirty years old.

Her appearance would be acceptable for being white for people who didn't know she was a negro. She had a very attractive figure and wore tight fitting clothes to show her waist line. Her smile was radiant and at one glance into her eyes could captivate any man. She was Mattie's mother and was in charge of the big house, and was a clean fanatic who absolutely would not tolerate anything dirty throughout the house.

She stood over six feet tall with beautiful long black hair that surpassed her waist line. It was a saying that she was the most beautiful woman in the world until Mattie came along. Younger white women felt Mama Sue's presence and felt insecure, and they were jealous of her, because of her beauty still holding on. As for Bonnie McKinley, Young Master McKinley's mother had a serious thing for field hand slaves. She liked to make love to them because they did it while frightened to death. She also liked the smell of their stink and to feel the muscles of the field hand slaves. So, she spent many nights visiting the slave's quarters. She was aesthetic with black slaves. She would always say the blacker the berry the sweeter the juice. Possibly that's where that saying started. Her life was very secretive, and she would do anything to be with a slave. Young Master McKinley knew all about his mother's secrets. But, would do everything within his power to protect her.

Mattie was a sight to see, she was always calm and relaxed with the most beautiful smile the world had ever seen. Her hair and clothes were always neat. Some said that she was the prettiest girl in Mississippi. So beautiful and eloquent until it caught the eyes of many white men that came into contact with her. Many fell in love with her with just one look. Mattie was Master

McKinley's lover ever since she was ten years old. Master McKinley had fallen so deep in love with Mattie over the years until he allowed her to share with her mother in running the entire household as if she was his wife, which she later became. Even though she was considered a house slave, she was never treated as a slave.

Master McKinley never cared about what whites thought. No one interfered in his life. Mattie had control over the house and yard slaves as if she was a white woman.

Oscar's birth was unusual because of the color of his hair and eyes. No one had ever seen or heard of a biracial woman giving birth to a blonde-haired green-eyed baby that was considered to be a negro. His father Master James Williams McKinley named his son Oscar McKinley, but immediately nicknamed him, Eyes, because of how beautiful his deep green eyes were. They mesmerized all the people who saw them. He even demanded people to call Oscar Eyes, because they were so beautiful.

The conversation was always about how crystal green his eyes were, upon seeing him for the first time. All whites admired his looks and stated he had British blood along with a touch of Irish. Never speaking of his African bloodline. As the story goes Oscar could pass for a white man. Mattie started out as a house negro that grew up in the Big House. Her job was making up beds and laundry. Something she attended to until she was twelve.

Young Master McKinley had started visiting Mattie in the middle of the night for sex at the age of ten. So, it was a well-kept secret, until Mattie became thirteen. Then other men begin to notice her fine figure. Mattie didn't mind showing it off and Master McKinley enjoyed seeing her do it.

He was aesthetic and intrigued and had tailor made clothes designed around Mattie's waist line. Plus, he would buy Mattie beautiful clothes every time he took her to a business meeting. She learned early what white men wanted to see and she concluded that it was her beautiful figure. Mattie was a sight to see, she was always calm and relaxed with one of the most beautiful smiles the world had ever seen. Her hair and clothes were always neat. Some said that she was the most beautiful girl in the world. So beautiful and eloquent until it caught the eyes of all the white men that came into contact with her. Many fell in love with her with just one look. She spoke with such confidence.

Master McKinley would challenge any white man to a dual to the death with pistols, if he heard or suspected any talk of Oscar being a negro or his biological mother sleeping with one.

He had killed seven white men in duals, and murder eight slaves including Mama Sue. The person who raised him. His mother was petrified that he would murder her. She was afraid to go to sleep at night. She kept slaves in her room at night barricading the door. Because she knew it was only a matter of time before Master McKinley would come for her. Sure, enough Master McKinley ordered Quick George to kill his own mother. That's how bad Master McKinley wanted his secret about Eyes kept. It was taking days for Quick George to Kill Ms. Bonnie. After a while Master McKinley noticed that Quick George was struggling to find a way to kill her. It shouldn't have been a problem, because Quick George had killed whites before at the request of Master McKinley.

His favorite choice was to poison them. Each passing day Master McKinley felt threatened by the fact that she knew about Eyes. So, he gave Quick George a direct order a second time to kill his mother as soon as possible. However, Quick George did not want to kill her. So, he came up with another Idea of making it look like Ms. Bonnie was dead. Quick George also lied to Master McKinley about the killing of Mama Sue. He stated that he had killed her and disposed of the body. So, he hatched a story of her moving to Britain to live in a cooler climate and took along Mama Sue, where it wasn't so hot. Quick George helped them to go into hiding. Leaving Master McKinley thinking that Quick George was the only one left knowing the secret about Eyes.

DANGER MAN

When Oscar (Eyes) turned fifteen years of age, he had more power than Master McKinley and was actually running the entire stables, which included everyone working with the horses, and he wasn't shy about delegating authority. Plus, he was one of the best horsemen in the world, if not the best. White men feared eyes, because they knew any cross words with eyes could mean getting fired or facing Master McKinley guns. All eyes had to do was tell Master McKinley that there was a problem. He would Immediately deal with the situation. He had a quick temper and the people in the county knew that Master McKinley was a very dangerous man, with thin patience for white men. He would even go as far as murdering white men who disrespected Eyes. Because he did not fear the law. Basically, because he practically was the law in the county and he knew that no Judge within the county would convict him. No matter what he did, because he owned two thirds of the county.

It was Master McKinley who decided how things were ran in the county, and he could change the laws, if necessary. He always bragged about Eyes being the best son ever. Both father and son shared a weakness for women. When Eyes turned sixteen years of age, he had women of several different races madly in love with him. Eyes had his share of romance with girls that were white, black, Mexican, Chinese and Indians. It all depended on the day of the week, the one he would choose.

Master McKinley wanted Eyes happy and anything Eyes wanted; Eyes got. Master McKinley often marveled at how much Eyes reminded him of his mother. He would sit and talk to Eyes about his mother for hours at a time. But there was one thing that Eyes always kept secret from Master McKinley. He knew that his mother was a negro, because Old Mama Sue had told him years earlier.

SLAVE OWNERS CRUSH

Master McKinley finished college and came after being away for two years. Upon his return he realized that Mattie had started a relationship with Mr. Smith's son Peter. The relationship started over a year ago in the absence of Young Master McKinley. Mr. Smith owned a large Plantation about fifty miles away. Mattie soon realized that Peter was actually in love with her and needed to see her on a regular basis. He would come over to visit The McKinley Plantation just to get a peek at Mattie and she loved the attention. Peter would request Mattie to get something for him and try his best to get Mattie alone. She would play all kinds of tricks to make sure he failed.

Old Master McKinley even begins to notice young Peter's strange visits, that often-turned-out seeking time with Mattie, while young Master Mckinley was away in college. Mattie had become flirty and began to see all white men as dogs in heat, except for Young Master McKinley, whom she loved. Mattie started requesting money and all types of things from Peter. She would even sneak out at night to meet him.

On several occasions Old Master McKinley would simply tell Peter to go home. Peter would plead with Master McKinley to sell him Mattie, but the answer was always the same, NO. But, somewhere during these times Old Master McKinley decided to sell Mattie to Peter. But young Master McKinley found out and came home. He had decided to kill his father in order to keep Mattie.

After a couple of years later Mattie was able to do things white girls couldn't do, like kiss a white boy in public places and walk down the streets holding hands. In fact, Mattie was freer than any other white woman in Mississippi. Young Master Mckinley wanted to keep it that way. He would kill any man who stood in his way that challenged his relationship with Mattie. He had six pistol duals with white men who didn't honor his relationship with Mattie. There was talk that Master McKinley had four other white men killed, because he heard that they had bad mouth Mattie. He had a violent temple and never cared about what others thought about race mixing. Master McKinley was a very dangerous man. He always kept many bodyguards around for protection of his lifestyle. He inherited The McKinley Plantation after he murdered Old Master McKinley. After receiving ownership, he Immediately started letting it be known how much he was attracted to biracial women. Young Master McKinley Often stated that biracial women were the most beautiful women in the world.

Nearly every slave owner that visited the McKinley Plantation made large offers to purchase Mattie. It was sort of strange, but Master McKinley liked seeing white men desire his slave girl. Yet and still, he was a jealous man that hated the men who wanted her. His psychopathic behavior was beginning to surface more by the day. In all actuality Master McKinley was a serial killer, who enjoyed killing men especially slave owners.

Any white man who showed Mattie too much attention ended up dead. He would eliminate the threat, by all means. Peter was found with a broken neck two days after Master McKinley returned. Master McKinley's love for Mattie went beyond race and laws of the land. He was going to marry Mattie. She was absolutely the love of his life. She dominated all men, especially Master McKinley. Whatever she wanted she got. She would never let Master McKinley touch her without first giving her something she wanted. She was very business oriented and it absolutely drove Master McKinley crazy. Most of her demands were outrageous, but Master McKinley always accommodated her. It only made him desire her more. He always respected her wishes, and worked hard at winning all her love. When Mattie became fourteen, she made a request that slaves were not allowed to do at that time.

She asked Master McKinley to marry her. Which was very strange for such a young slave girl. So, after a long-drawn-out winter, Master McKinley honored her request and married her in the Spring However, their marriage was kept a secret. Even though there were white and black people who knew. They wouldn't dare speak of such things, because they knew that it would cost them their life. No one got into his business.

Mattie was fourteen at the time and she was the prettiest girl anyone had ever laid eyes upon. She carried herself in an eloquent way and always spoke with confidence using correct English. She spoke three different languages. Young Master McKinley had taught Mattie every single thing he knew, plus she had a tutor for all the subjects she liked. But Mattie was never satisfied with her knowledge and wanted to learn more. So, Master McKinley would buy books for her from almost every place he visited. Mattie was considered a genius.

SUPER STAR

Master McKinley would always save his best horse and rider for the big money races. His main horse in all the big races was a horse named Memphis and the rider was always Eyes. He would always say that the only rider that could ever beat Eyes would be him (jokingly). People would always laugh. Eyes knew that slaves were the best riders to win a horse race.

But Eyes always rode in the big money races. Over the years Eyes had become more famous than Master McKinley. Eyes was the first superstar athlete in America. The same as today's Patrick Mahomes. All races of people loved him. There were also rumors circulating among the slaves that Eyes was a black angel sent directly from heaven to save the slaves. The field slaves would run and hide near the big house to get a glimpse of Eyes as he rode past. Field hand slave girls all dreamed of someday meeting Eyes, strange, but some of them were in love with the thought of marrying Eyes. Eyes were their super hero.

Some compared Eyes to Moses from the Old Testament. Because he was kind and had a special likeness for slaves. Eyes was also a member of the underground railroad helping many slaves escape from the south and go north. The McKinley Plantation had several escape routes to Canada. Eyes didn't approve of slavery and often didn't try to hide it. Strangely, Master McKinley had the same philosophy. Yet he owned slaves. Eyes actually made a lot of white men rich, so they could buy more slaves. Which was something he hated. Most white men worshiped Eyes and never paid attention to what he did. They would even present their daughter's hand in marriage to Eyes, on many occasions.

However, Eyes was focused on winning horse races, and getting as many slaves to freedom as he possibly could. Eyes thought his underground railroad work was his greatest kept secret, but Master McKinley Knew every move Eyes made and, on many occasions, he would assist Eyes, without him knowing. He simply didn't care about anything that made Eyes feel unhappy. All he wanted was for Eyes to be happy. Sometimes Master McKinley would help his own slaves escape. Eyes never suspected his father of helping his own slaves escape. It was a bond between the two that no one could break. Master McKinley loved Eyes more than anything else in the world.

Eyes were well liked. Plus he was the most famous athlete in the world. Little white boys would follow him around in hope of getting notice and a chance to shake his hand. White girls would shout and scream in his presence. People came from miles just to see Eyes in a horse race. No one in America had ever been as popular. However poor whites heard the rumors that Eyes was a negro and wanted so badly to get their hands on him. They wanted to lynch him. It didn't go unnoticed by Master McKinley, so everywhere Eyes went in public there were two white and two black men that went along. Master McKinley would say it was to keep Eyes from spending too much money, but the people knew they were his bodyguards.

Eyes wasn't shy about telling the men what to do either, so it was easy for people to see who was in charge. He could tell the cooks what he wanted to eat and they had to prepare it as fast as possible or Master McKinley became angry and punished anyone who denied his request. Eyes were treated as one would treat a King. By the time Eyes was sixteen, he truly had become the best rider the world has ever seen. He was the first ever to use the monkey crouch. He realized that his weight didn't affect the horse's stride in the monkey crouch. People would laugh at Eyes the way he rode, but it always gave him an advantage over the other riders. It helped Eyes to win every race. Eyes only rode in the big money races and his horse was named Memphis. Master McKinley would always say that the only rider that could ever beat Eyes would be him (jokingly). People would always laugh. Eyes knew that slaves were the best riders to win a horse race. Because they were hungry to win and earn their freedom. So, he had all slave riders, along with slave trainers. Because he knew slaves wanted to do better than a white man. So, he gave them that chance, because he felt slaves would put forth more effort into winning.

THE CON

Master McKinley would always bet huge amounts of money on the race of his choice. But the big money had to be on a horse Eys was riding, and most of the time that horse was Memphis. Master McKinley had many trades, but the one that went unnoticed the most, was Master McKinley being a con man, who made millions of dollars dishonestly in horse races. It didn't matter to him if he cheated or not, all he wanted was more money and he loved making money.

He would race slower horses against the visitor's best and this horse would always lose the first two races. He would have horses that looked exactly alike, or he would have Quick George paint them. Quick George was an old biracial slave who could draw and paint anything his eyes came upon.

He was one of the world's greatest painters, so it wasn't a problem for him to make one horse look exactly like another. The con usually came in after losing several races Master McKinley would complain about his black slave rider not being smart enough to see the correct moves in those particular races.

Alright, the con was in, then he would take another horse that looked exactly like the losing horse, and explain that his white son could get the job done better.

He would then triple the amount and Eyes would bring the horse in every time. Eyes invented the rider standing up, and no one else in the world rode like Eyes. He was by far the best rider in the world with international experience and he only rode Master McKinley's best horses. He would only enter a race when the stakes were high. Sometimes worth more than a million dollars. Eyes spent plenty of his money buying lavish gifts for women that he liked. It didn't matter if she was married or not. Eyes did whatever he desired, with the backing of Master McKinley. Eyes would simply send her a message usually by Quick George. He would send her a gift or sometimes cash. But, always one or the other. The meeting place was then set up, and it was usually in a wagon that Eyes always travel with to entertain women. The women always showed up. Eyes would have his way as always.

Married plantation women gave Eyes the time of his life. But whenever one fell in love with him, he would always discontinue the relationship. Eyes would then give each woman the same speech, I love you too, good bye.

THE SNEAKY PLAN

Master McKinley hatched a plan that would get him out of the plantation business for good. Because it was something that he hated being a part of, he felt that owning people was wrong. So, one day Master McKinley met a man named Mr. Deal Maker, who explained to him that he knew of a Prince who was the richest man in the world. He stated that The Prince would cover any bet, anyone would have the nerves to bet on a horse race. It was something that got Master McKinley's undivided attention. He saw an opportunity to get out of the slavery business once and for all. Mr. Deal Maker explained that the prince made most of his money on horse races.

The prince claimed that his horses were the best in the world. So, Master McKinley asked Mr. Deal Maker to invite the prince to The McKinley Plantation, and for him to bring his best horses and plenty of gold to bet. Because he had the fastest horses in the world and was ready to prove it against anyone. Master McKinley was willing to bet everything he had on his best horse named "Memphis". So, Mr. Deal Maker sent for the prince. Master McKinley assured Mr. Deal Maker that he would cover any bet the price could make. Because he wanted the title of being the richest man in the world. So, after six months had passed the prince arrived from Saudi Arabia loaded with diamonds, gold, and rubies, with some of the finest horses one had ever seen.

The exception was Master McKinley had several horses that looked as good or better. It was a horse named "Memphis", and another named "Solid Good". The prince brought his horse's special grain from Saudi Arabia which energize them to run faster and it also made their coats shine beautifully. It was an understanding during this time that gentlemen would always run their best horse last and make the largest bet on that particular race. Sometimes they would go broke, going all in on their best horse. Master McKinley's was sure his best horse was "Memphis' '. However, Eyes felt that Memphis had gotten too old and wasn't the best horse anymore. He felt that Solid Gold was now the fastest horse in the world. The problem was, Solid Gold didn't have enough experience in a big money race. This made Master McKinley leery of Solid Gold. Even though she had clocked the fastest time. It didn't deter Master McKinley away from Memphis. Plus, Memphis was encouraging and had never lost a race.

But there was no one in the world who knew horses better than Eyes, and Master McKinley had never questioned Eye's decision making before, when it came down to horses. Except this particular time. Master McKinley felt that he had too much wealth riding on the race to go with a new horse.

He wanted to go with a horse that had proven himself. So, for the first time in Master McKinley's life he separated himself from Eyes. He went against Eyes, and got his next best rider to ride Memphis. Because Eyes chose Solid Gold over Memphis. Master Mckinley would not listen to Eyes. He was adamant about his decision to run Memphis. Eyes felt betrayed because he was the only one that had been making the decisions on which horse would run in a particular race. He had a stable full of good horses, but only for a certain distance. So, he didn't feel that Memphis was strong enough for the chosen distance. Plus, Eyes knew that no other horse in the world could beat Solid Gold and he would bet his life on the race. Because he was the world's greatest horseman. Even though Memphis was getting old, he was still considered a good horse and could probably win the race.

Except Eyes wanted to be sure, and he felt there would be no doubt riding Solid Gold. Together they were the best horse and rider in the world and no one could beat them on the planet. However, Memphis was known as the fastest horse in America, maybe the world. But Eyes knew Solid Gold could beat Memphis. So, he felt that she should be first in line as their best horse. Plus, Eyes was afraid to take Memphis through the extreme training. Because Memphis was aging fast and could easily die during the training. He didn't want anything to happen to Memphis because Memphis was his favorite horse. Eyes would often sleep in the stables with Memphis, just to be near him because he loved him so much.

THE MILLION DOLLAR RACE

The race would be in three weeks. Eyes started sleeping every night he could in Solid Gold's stall. Because Eyes had chosen Solid Gold to run in the big race. But Master McKinley disagreed and snuck and changed the race date to two weeks without Eyes knowing. He even got a slave named Toby to ride Memphis behind Eyes back. A rider Eyes felt was too aggressive. Plus, he knew Eyes would never agree on Memphis being the best horse at the time and he only trusted Memphis. Going against Eyes made Master McKinley angry with himself. He directed his anger toward white men. A group he hated for owning slaves, so he took pleasure in killing them. It was something he believed was the right thing to do, because he hated slave owners.

So, two days before the big race Master McKinley sent Eyes fifty miles away driving a wagon to pick up more gold needed to bet on the race against the prince, with Eyes under the Impression that the race was one week away. Plus, such a trip would take at least three days. Well, as soon as Eyes left. They begin getting the track ready for the big race the very next day. Master McKinley was so sure Memphis would win, he put up all the Gold and cash he had on hand.

The people placed their largest bets on Memphis. Master McKinley had Quick George dope up Memphis doing the night before the race. So, he would be extremely fast. Which was a mistake because Memphis hadn't received the training needed for such a race. Eyes were concentrating on getting Solid Gold ready for race day. Therefore, leaving Memphis unprepared. So, The Prince put up large amounts of gold and rubies. In order to match his bet Master McKinley had to put up The McKinley Plantation along with the big house and all his slaves. That meant all of his beautiful slave girls and yard slaves could be sold off into the hands of wicked slave owners. The tragedy was Memphis died in the middle of the race. Most of the people who bet on Memphis lost large sums of money, because they had never seen Memphis lose a race. Memphis was usually a sure thing, except for this time. The people became angry with Master McKinley, stating that he ran a sick horse. Poor Master McKinley was left owning only his horse stable.

Several men made death threats that same day. Master McKinley walked up to those men and shot them dead, right in front of the entire crowd. No one said a word out of fear. Because they knew that Master McKinley was a serial killer and was in the killing mood. The sheriff witnesses the shooting. He claimed that both men were armed and had threatened the life of Master McKinley. So, he had no choice but to defend himself. One day afterwards Eyes returned with the gold. The prince and his guest were still there. The news had gotten to Eyes and he returned as fast as possible. Master McKinley started to cry in front of other men. He was talking about committing suicide, and had a hand gun in his hand, when Eyes showed up. Even though Eyes felt badly about the death of Memphis. He loved Master McKinley so much more and couldn't Imagine living without him. Immediately Eyes began to plead with Master McKinley to not hurt himself and that he forgave him. After a lengthy conversation with Eyes. Master McKinley asked The Prince for another race, and this time everything he owned was on the line. His claim was Memphis wasn't his best horse. So, the Prince jumped at the offer for another race to beat his best horse.

Because he wanted to beat Master McKinley's best horse along with his best rider. He wanted to beat Eyes. So, The Prince put up large amounts of gold and rubies. Eyes forgot about all the gold and silver he was riding for; he could only think about getting back the Great McKinley Plantation along with the house and yard slaves.

So, the race was set for three days later. Solid Gold was a short red filly with big booming eyes. She could never stand still for long, and always bobbed her head around. She was fiery and exciting to watch, at times it was as though she was having a conversation with Eyes. It was clear that they were a team and ready to do battle. Master McKinley had seen the prince horse run and felt that Solid Gold had no chance of winning. But Eyes wanted to clean out the prince and it was all or nothing. The day of the race Eyes had changed clothes with a field hand slave. He was smelly and had on rags for clothes, dressed exactly as a field hand.

It was Eyes expressing his roots and he wanted to look exactly as a slave. Right away Master McKinley knew Eyes knew that he was a slave. It was something he never wanted Eyes to know. But in some strange way he became prouder of eyes, because he loved his mother so much.

One of the townspeople called him out as a slave. Immediately Master McKinley walked over and held a short conversation with the man then shot him in the head. That was the end of that talk.

There were three horses in this particular race. Another horse had arrived from New York and he was fast. It appeared that the prince feared him and not Solid Gold. The race started with three horses. Solid Gold was so short until she looked like a pony standing beside the other horses. When the race started Solid Gold hesitated and fell behind. Eyes didn't panic, he let her set her pace. He was a very experienced rider. Around the halfway marker Solid Gold decided she wanted to catch up, then Eyes turned her loose and she ran like lightning. It was a beautiful sight; Solid Gold was shining in the sunlight with a gallop so strong and steady, some said it was the most beautiful thing they had ever seen.. It was easy to say that this horse was the best horse in the world, along with the best rider. Eyes rode a perfect race and coasted to the win. Master Mckinley regained all that was lost and more. He had won enough money to reimburse his associates who lost money on Memphis. At least he thought he did. But there was a catch. Master McKinley had put up the title of the land to the winner. So, in the second race he was expecting to see the title back on the line. But the prince didn't have it. Because it was Illegal for an Arab to own land and slaves in America. So, the two men who bought the land from the prince couldn't legally own it. Because by law the land still belongs to Master McKinley. The two men went into hiding. Three days later Master McKinley got shot in the back and two days later passed away. It all turned out to be a big mess.

The two men claim to have bought the land from Master McKinley before the race. This was not true. But it became a battle in the courts. The struggle to get back the land went on for years. Eyes became violent just like his father. Any mention of him being a negro meant death for that particular person.

Many people were killed. It had gotten to a point where the McKinley's had to go into hiding. They were hated within the county, because of all their relatives being killed by Master McKinley. So, they formed a group called the peace riders and began to hunt and kill all McKinley's. Yet, legally the McKinley's still owned the land.

EQUALITY
PART THREE

Everybody at the table was quiet and listening to dad and his twin brother tell the most fascinating story. Then, all of a certain both men turned to me, stating that I was named after the legend of the family. They both seemed concerned about me living up to the name of my slave owning great, great, great grandfather. Immediately, I stood up from the table before I knew it. The first thing that came out of my mouth was that he was wrong, but we are rich and I want every penny back. So, I'm going to fix it dad, and get our money back. I didn't exactly understand what I was saying. But later understood it to be some type of reparations. Because I interpreted the story as the family master's father and son's greatest desire was for all men to live equally. Yes, I replied, I will uphold the name of The McKinley's. It was a burden that was thrusted upon me at the age of ten.

The story empowered me. I felt destined to do great things involving race equality. My siblings looked at me as though I had accepted a mission Impossible. I knew it would be tough with a watered-down education from Mississippi. A black person in Mississippi couldn't even go to a library. Because it was against the law. I heard a story of a little girl trying to enter the library, who got hit with a policeman stick and went into a coma and later died. So, I knew, that I would have to come from the back of the pack. Because I couldn't get a proper education in Mississippi.

All of a certain I felt the weight of the world on my shoulders. I felt so insufficient and began to wonder, how was I going to get educated enough to achieve such a task. Right then, I started to understand that I would have to leave Mississippi for good. I realized that my dad had been guiding me toward this special task all along. It also came up that dad was my real dad and not my step dad. It was something that I thought I would never hear; my dad was a white man. But I always had my suspicions all along. But it didn't seem to matter anymore. I loved my dad no matter his race and I knew he loved me, my siblings and mother, and she was a black woman. He had a special kindness in his heart for black people. He was a wonderful human being.

We were struggling together to bring about equality helping the poor. I took on a portion of that responsibility in first grade at the age of five. I used to give my lunch money away so other kids could eat. I thought every little bit helped. But I had no idea where to start with such a large task. I only knew it had to be done and I would play a large role in bringing it to pass. I was only ten years old at this time, but the force inside of me was strong. From that day forward I was aware of the seriousness of the race problems in Mississippi. I made a pledge to my family that night that I would personally play a role in getting reparations for slavery in America and Africa. I started approaching the world differently and began to notice things, like the privileges whites had over blacks. It made me feel uncomfortable and embarrassed. Just knowing my family was once the richest family in Mississippi was too much to swallow.

I concluded that whites were suppressing the truth on many fronts, and I needed to expose it. I knew I needed to learn as much as I could about each race. But I couldn't find the books in Mississippi to help me learn what I needed to know. It became clear to me that my task would require a superb education, which is the reason I left Mississippi to basically get a decent education. The laws in the southern states stated that blacks were not allowed to enter any library in any of the southern states. I heard horror stories about blacks being beaten and jail, just trying to enter a library and learn. There was no way to be equal in knowledge, because of the laws that suppress blacks. So, I fell short of a proper education. I used to lay in my bed at night, sometimes crying and praying. Just for an opportunity to go to the library. So, when I hear the slogan make America great again. I think of a time when we had the races separated. One area for the color and another for the white. I'm sure that's what they're saying.

Aww, but when I did get a chance in the northern states. I stayed in the library night and day. It was so much fun learning. God sent me through religion, sociology, psychology to special education. There were several philosophers that were attracting my attention. But Jesus was the strongest force in my life, so I ended up in bible college. I had a black friend there who had just about every book that was written by Dr. Martin L King, or about him. I started reading those books and I learned Dr. King was dealt a serious short hand from the whites as well. But he actually did something about it. Which was something that was in my planning. During that time. However, I knew more about Billy Graham than Dr. King at the time. In fact I knew more about him than anyone else at the bible college, especially the professors. Billy Graham had my attention for a while. But once I started reading about Dr. King, it was like being sucked up into the Starship Enterprise. His struggle was my srtruggle.

There was a time in my life, I would read something about Dr. King before I went to bed and the first thing I read was something about Dr. King the very next day. He helped me on my journey; however, psychology aided me as well. He crossed over and so did I. Once you've crossed, you begin to know what you know. You're not trying to figure out things, because you begin to see things crystal clear.

I started up where Dr. King left off. That year I did something at that school that had never been done before. I became President of the student body and made it my business to speak in the chapel on Dr. King's birthday. I rocked it. Well, it was Dr. Martin Luther King Jr, Billy Graham, along with Leonardo da Vinci who gave me a rock-hard foundation. It really wasn't all the things they said, it was more of how they did things. But that was just the beginning, because God works through personalities. He wanted me to know about many more extraordinary people.

Mainly Jesus. So, I would know what's clicking in me. The hardest part was learning ways to express what was inside of me. Because my personality was so different from each of these men. However, I had one thing that stood out and it was comedy. I liked being funny, making people laugh was rewarding, because it made me feel good. However, I started out as this funny, yet serious preacher, but somewhere along the line. I moved away from preaching because psychology drew my attention. But I still held on to Jesus and realized they both went together.

I had attended at least three different colleges before starting school at MidAmerica Nazarene University in Olathe Kansas to achieve my B.A. in religion with a minor in psychology. At that time, it was the best school in Kansas. My classmates were 97% white. I had a habit of turning in my paper first on test day, usually making the highest score. No one seemed to ever score higher than me in most of my classes. But sometimes I ended up with the wrong Instructor and they created problems and would not give me an A. These teachers liked giving completions on a test, that way they could easily take points away, and I almost never got full credit. Yet I usually made A's. I knew some of the students that got a few better grades than I did on occasions. But I was by far the best student on campus. Definitely the best Greek student that ever went there.

Dr. Richard Spindle was a white man from Texas. He was my favorite teacher. He went on to become the President of MidAmerica Nazarene University. We were friends, who took many walks during the lunch hour. I would sometimes miss my lunch to take that walk. We would talk about a variety of things. He was sort of like a father figure. Sometimes other teachers would tag alone. Boy, did I get into some heated arguments with them, but never him. He would sometimes tell us to stop and I always stopped as soon as he gave me the word. Sometimes they kept talking, but I stopped responding. They could never figure out our relationship. We just had respect for one another. The funny thing about that was, they would then become angry at the two of us, every time he told me to stop. I guess because I wouldn't listen to them under any circumstances, and they hated that. He was my mentor at the time along with being a friend. We could talk to each other about anything. Every morning when I arrived at school, I went straight to his office to have my morning coffee. He always welcomed me and I was delighted to see him.

He was the chair of the department and he taught philosophy (loved it). He was one of the best friends that I have ever had. He was a silent warrior. Yet powerful. He would always encourage me, and on rare occasions he would express what a great person I was. I believed every word he said, most of the time. He talked to me the same way my dad did. I felt comfortable around him. He was such a wonderful man. I learned from him how the devil operated in politics. He was trying to resolve the race problem in America as well as I.

He warned me not to get entangled with the spotlight. Because then all I could do was chase after the shining objects. He helped me to understand the Importance of staying clear of the attention seekers, and to find some of the books I needed to read. I found lots of world secrets hidden in Catholic and Muslim books. He always told me not to read them, but I did. The thing was tracking them down and which library had the correct information. I used to order books from many places in the world. Those books gave me clues here and there. But I still had to put it all together for myself. Well, that's one gift God gave me, the wisdom to connect different parts of history. I was aligning myself directly into the path of how to untangle the race problems in America and around the world. Above all, how to get reparations for slavery.

THE NEED FOR REPARATIONS FOR SLAVERY

We must never forget about slavery. However, we must keep spreading the love of Jesus. It's the right thing to do, but keep denouncing evil. I'm uniquely connected to you, but I'm going to defy my philosophy about my intrinsic qualities and make a confession today that has been long overdue. A lot of you already know, but never speak of it and you should. I think it's time now. It has been yours truly who have been the voice crying out, saying repent white America and do reparation for slavery, and for all the other setbacks that your states and federal government have thrusted upon poor black people.

Only a reparation settlement is the answer. America must do it and Kamala Harris is the one to do it. I'm the true prophet, by the will of God. I understand the Scriptures well, about the lady touching Jesus' garment. She came from behind Jesus in the crowd and touched his garment. Jesus immediately turned to his disciples and asked the question who touched me. No one answered, everyone denied touching him, but Jesus stated that someone had deliberately touched him because he felt the power go out of him. That Scriptures have taught me many things about Jesus and it's still teaching me how to understand the power of Jesus. I can somewhat relate to that. I feel America, because every time I write I feel power going out of me.

On one hand how many roads must a man walk down, before he can see. On the other hand, how many rivers must he cross before he can hear what the new beat says, rock and roll with me. You don't have to ask yourself if you believe in miracles. Because, if you believe in me, I'm your miracle and I will prove it to you, so stand on it. America needs the truth. The question is, what should America do about the insane abuse thrusted upon poor black people from slavery They have to correct the slavery problem now, in order for America to look like a civilized nation. Things have fallen apart with Donald Trump. Reparation is needed for at least 10 different setbacks, so take your pick.

The Idea of slavery was predicated on an assumption that black Americans are inferior and always have been inferior to whites, and that systemic inequality must exist because of them being inferior to whites. That's not true, unless God did not create all men equal. So, we're tired of the insane lies, and the suffering being overlooked. The longer we wait the greater the divide becomes. We must move forward now and pay blacks for slavery. Because all of America suffers from the embarrassment of slavery. Not fixing it has gone on too long. There's no place to hide anymore and book banding is cruel. Slavery will always be there until it's fixed. It's a dirty shame and needs to be fixed now. All Christian know that.

Kamala Harris could go down in history as the number one president. If not number one for sure number two. All she has to do is reparations for slavery. She has already shown us how she can get things done. Plus, she has the heart of a lion. She's the only President who has the greatest opportunity to do it, because the country is ready to put reparations behind us. We're tired of the craziness of Donald Trump and his brain washed followers. They are lawless. After it's done, it may only take Kamala Harris 10 years later for her to become the number one President of the United States of America and she will remain there as long as America exists. The greatest President of all time will be Kamala Harris.

Now, there are two black men in Georgia in a southern state, running for the US Senate. It's so beautiful and unique, cuter than Santa Claus. I think I'll stay on the sidelines this time. Because Georgia is too sweet, plus I love eating peaches. It's too interesting for me to get involved. Only one will win the race, but they are both winners. So, let freedom ring from Stone Mountain in Georgia, because it's long overdue. Now, racism is wrong people, let me say it again, racism is wrong, so denounce it. Because it takes away the beauty of God's creation. Love is the answer and it's at the other end of control. No man is capable of processing the dynamics involved unless God reveals its secrets. You won't get it through hate. I'm 100% positive. GOD WANTS REPARATION FOR SLAVERY SO AMERICA CAN HEAL.

Here's our song "Teddy Pendergrass - Somebody Told Me (Official Audio)"

Now, there is a need for reparation not only for American blacks, but for African blacks as well. Because the European countries owe Africa reparation for constantly stealing their wealth. It's so embarrassing to see the destitute and actually be a witness of the destructive path left behind by the white Europeans and it's so evil and out of control. Oh, let me add this. There is no such thing as The Royal Family in Britain they are only thefts expressing white supremacy over black African people. It needs to stop, now. It's all an act of greed.

Now, one other thing about the Georgia senate race. I don't care what kind of education Herschel Walker has, it's totally Irrelevant. Alright let's learn. One third of our beloved Presidents were uneducated and half of them were called our greatest Presidents. That's no surprise to me but maybe to you. People are caught up on who has the best education. Don't get me wrong, education is a good thing, but at times it can be a curse. Not everyone needs a degree. Ivy league schools. WHAT'S THAT? Maybe it's the white man's mirage, or simply displaying a condescending attitude toward blacks and women. Because blacks and women were not meant to attend Ivy League schools.

Alright, that title should not be used anymore. It's racist. Slave's owner profited off Ivy League schools more so than any other schools. That's what made them so advanced. Why should they be considered as good schools? They made profits off of slavery, which degraded blacks. The schools are grand, and they all owned black people, sort of like another slave big house. Now white people have to get away from those Illusions in order for America to become great. Alright. Here's our song "Brothers Going to Work it Out - Willie Hutch." Now, when people have the power of God working in their lives. They can do great unexplained things without monkeying around embedded in evil works. Like making the Impossible seem easy. I didn't recognize how great God's power within me was, until I saw President Barack Obama in trouble. I knew then that there was no one else on earth who could save him, except for me. So, I saved him from the hands of the devilish Republican Party. Next thing I knew, the Republicans were trying to steal Obamacare. I didn't want that, so God sent me back in, to stop it, and I did. I did it alone with the help of God's Spirit. The Spirit helped me to influence the right people. I saved Obamacare. That might be something that made America great. One thing I have learned, and that is God's power is only active for the goodness of mankind. It's not selfish and desires greed. OK. Right now, watch the world change as I write. The world is mine and it's awaiting me. But I have good patience and I'm more concerned about humanizing the world, than the spotlight. I'm the epitome of what Jesus' love represents. Yes, Dr. Oscar McKinley saved Obamacare. His work Saved millions of American lives along with the economy. Thoughts on the American Presidency is about saving Obamacare, and it's a book I wrote. I could have changed the results of Donald Trump's impeachment trial and it all ended there. But God wanted hearts to be exposed. So, he could change race relations for good. End racism once and for all. So, God didn't ask me to get deeply involved in Donald Trump and the Republicans crazy lunatic mess. Because God is love, not confusion. They have backed themselves into a corner, and it's now Impossible to escape their wicked ways. They are possessed with doing the devil's work. They must be accountable to God. Alright. There's no way for them to please God anymore. They have sold their soul to the devil and can now only produce evil. Because evil cannot produce love.

FACEBOOK POLITICIAN
PART FOUR

Some years later, I started using the most powerful tool in the world which was Facebook. Writing articles and posting them. I never got many likes, but I knew people were reading my postings. Facebook gave me an opportunity to express everything I had learned throughout the years. On most occasions I was writing directly to the oppressor and the oppressed, because I knew they would sooner or later catch on to the gravity of my writings. I knew Americans liked to read. However, there were other countries involved in the deception who liked reading as well. So, I broaden my writings to include the world. Because history had completely been falsified, making a fool out of the whites as well as the blacks. So, I started teaching and expressing true history in my writings.

Most people had no Idea what I was talking about. Even the smart people were struggling most of the time. So, I took my time teaching. It was like teaching first graders, all beginners. So, I went slow and was very patient and caring. People begin to picked up on my writing after years of slow walking. Before I knew it, all races were reading my writings. No more slow walking needed.

Hollywood and television took a shining to it, along with women and the news channels. On some occasions the scholars were lost as well. What I was presenting was new to the world. It made people take a second look in the mirror. I did the work like Indiana Jones (the movie). Except, I'm real and he was a fictitious character. I must admit I was seeking out Information as he was at the time of his first Indiana Jones movie. Also, a television show called 'Matlock' was exhilarating and quite motivating to watch. Because, I could equate my life-style alongside his. I was working hard to resolve factors in life involving the races of people. While Matlock cracked the most difficult crime cases. I was tracking down things in the history of the church. So, by watching the show it motivated me to keep attacking the most difficult race problems in America, as well as the world. I had to teach people about their races, especially the black and white race. They did not know history and who they really were. It was like solving a case. You had to collect all evidence, sometime in the least ex-pected places. I learned it was very difficult for the white race to understand that all they had learned were mostly lies. Because the facts show that there have been more African kings ruling throughout Europe, than white Euro-peans. They even had black kings in Britain during the slave trade. Yes, King James was a black man. Yeah, he's the one who had the bible translated into English. It's the bible blacks and whites love. Yeah, most of the races had no Idea he was a black man. Black Kings ruled Europe from it existence, all the way up to the last black king, which was King George. Whites didn't know that, neither did blacks as well as the rest of the world. It was dangerous discussing the facts about it. Neither did they know that Jesus and Santa Clause were black. They begin to take a second look in the mirror. It was vitally Important for those two races to learn. So, they could stop making a fool out of themselves.

I was turning out to be the best computer Politician in the world. I knew at times I was one of the most powerful people on the planet. My knowledge could dominate any part of the world on any given day. If it was something I wanted to change in the world. I changed it right away, sometimes I waited until the last moments, but I posted the game changer. Sometimes it took time. However, overtime I was still able to change it. I would post my writings on Facebook. To me Facebook has the greatest connection to Intelligent people more so than any other device, including television. In my studying I read all of the great philosophers old and new. They were all brilliant people. But God gave me gifts that he didn't give them. Don't get me wrong, they were smart. But what separates me from them is my wide range of knowledge. I learned the races struggles and, in some ways. I must admit that I have learned more about the white race than any other race. Because it was part of my mission. They have created the greatest deception. Things like them being called white people. I found out that it only started three hundred years ago, and its purpose was to unify people who looked alike (albinism). Creating the trend for white supremacy. The beginning of the morons.

Also, we know Britain is the mother country of America. But there is a lot about Britain that we don't know. It's a shame how the world has been deceived by the so-called white race. King George III was the king who sent troops to America to free the slaves during The Revolutionary war. Yes, King George III was a black man. I know it's a shocker that King George was black. But so were all the Generals in the British Army. They were surprised to see American slaves fighting against them. It's time for the truth, America. It will bring love and peace. In fact, blacks have ruled the world for thousands of years. Whites have only ruled for the last two hundred years and have distorted history. So, all the Kings and Queens of England courts were filled with blacks. Americans copied their mannerisms. Knowledge is the truth and it's the path that God has chosen for us to follow.

The Bible states that fools run from knowledge. Let me add this. The main reason whites in America made the decision to enslave blacks was to try to avoid being ruled all over again by blacks, who might align themselves with black rulers of Europe. Now, the lies and secrets that eventually spread throughout the world were done by British and American writers. They all expounded on blacks being inferior. They begin to erase all history of the black kings and replace them with fake white men. It took me nearly twenty years to piece these things together, because it was hidden knowledge during that time. Now this same knowledge is accessible to whoever seeks the truth, it will set you free once and for all. Because the truth is the only thing that will set people free. Fabrication is a NO-NO. It's like a dog returning to eat his own vomit.

So, I'm going to keep it real and get down to the nitty-gritty, meaning the whole truth and nothing but the truth. Because ninety percent of what people have learned about the world is false and flat out lies. So, let's bypass sinister overtones. Starting with the rulers of the world. Let's go back to the days of Egypt and learn about the Great Pharaohs. First of all, Egypt is not one of the older countries of Africa, even though Egypt goes back thousands of years. In other words when Egypt became a country it was only through the support of Sudan. As always, a country starting out needs a mother country to lay the foundation. Sudan was their mother country and it set up rulership. All of the

Pharaohs came from Sudan and they were both African countries with all black people. This took place in Africa thousands of years before the birth of Jesus. There were no white Jewish slaves enslaved by black Sudanese and Egyptians. That's lie one, they were all black people and Christianity was only practiced in Africa during this time. Christianity is really an African religion. There are a lot of Arabs living there now, but they didn't arrive in Egypt until nearly a thousand years AD, with a different religion. So, they are not the original Egyptians, they are invaders.

Also, the Palestine people living in the middle east, who are calling themselves Jews are Arabs and are not Jewish people. Therefore, Jesus could not have been a brown man (Lie two). To be factual the so-called white Jew didn't lighten up until somewhere around seven or eight hundred years AD, and it happened in Russia and Germany (lie 3- white Jesus-impossible). That's why Hitler was so familiar. He knew the history of the Jews. Now let's talk about America and how this country was formed. As I stated, countries throughout the world always started with a mother country, even America. Britain was our mother country. Rulership was set up as in Britain except it was replaced by a black President instead of a King. Since the black Kings of Britain were still active and had rulership of America.

The first rulers here in America were black as well. All white males voted unanimously for a permanent line of black presidents starting with John Hanson, who was the first black President of the United States. He was followed by a line of other black Presidents. Another secret kept from history. They all came before George Washington. We need to get this straightened out. Because being dumb does not serve any good purpose, except for being stupid. George Washington only became President after the black generals of Britain were defeated by the American slaves, Only then could a white man become President and be accepted. George Washington was the first white President ever on the face of the earth to rule a so-called civilized nation, and he learned from black Presidents that came before him in America. White people in America feared the black kings of Europe and tried to appease them with black rulers. WHY? Because, it was traditionally accepted for rulership to look like the rulers of the mother country. All kings of Europe were black.

White men were not allowed to rule. They were not recognized on the world stage. Now, keep in mind no white man had ever ruled over a civilized nation before. George Washington was the first to try but slavery made him look uncivilized. The world believed that whites could never learn to be civilized. White men couldn't deal with the rest of the world. So, after the Revolutionary war America was free of the black kings of Europe and decided to go with a white president instead of another black. If you study George Washington closely, you'll realize he wasn't all that smart, he relied on the knowledge of the slaves, they were his main fighting force. He was just an old southern country boy, who had respect and truly believed in slaves. Slaves won that war for America. Alright, here's my song "10. The Impressions - This is My Country.

People ask me why I don't write more books instead of articles. I write more articles and not books because most people will never read a book. Unless they're in school. But they will read an article. You know people are predictable and mostly follow a trend of traditionalism. Not me. All I ever really wanted was knowledge and more knowledge, because Knowledge is a weapon. But you have to train diligently to be effective. I got saved relatively young. But it was always a struggle in and out of church until it dawned on me. The Scriptures explained why Christian's error. It's because of a lack of knowledge. So, I devoted my life to learning. I would read mostly anything I got my hands on, trying to be in step with God's Spirit. The bible says study to show yourself approved unto God. Plus, coming out of Mississippi learning from vintage books left me feeling insufficient. Sometimes I would read a book and study it night after night. I kept going until God okayed it. During some of those times I wasn't even in college. I would order certain books on many occasions and even call different priests overseas seeking knowledge, a clue here and there.

I found that reading Muslims and Catholic books were very rewarding and more closely related to what actually took place in the past. After a while knowledge starts empowering you. Those books usually gave true facts about the past better than Evangelical books. Evangelical books were usually off. I could find tampering. But let me tell you, it's one thing for sure, you still had to put it all together for yourself and that required a gift from God. Sometimes I marvel at what's in me that hasn't surfaced yet. Reading books gave me so much wisdom and a sense of peace. It was God getting me ready.

I believe God approved me. You have to study more than the bible to understand the bible. During that time, about thirty-five years ago, evangelicals were saying that Muslims and Catholics were practically devil worshippers. But I didn't let it scare me, I believed in God, and I wanted to know exactly why they were saying things like that about people that were worshiping the same God as Christian.

I basically learned that people haven't learned enough about each other's religion and customs, and they should, because it's the gate to the connection that's missing, creating a lack of knowledge. People are usually too busy trying to show others they're the one who's right and there is no room to compromise, set to fail.

AMERICA'S PROBLEM

There was always cool talk in Mississippi growing up about eating cheese. It carried a stigma that cheese eaters were snitchers. On that note I tried to avoid cheese. But I'm getting ready to expose the rot within the mental health field. As I have stated in many of my writings and radio shows that whites are fixated on dominating blacks and that mentality has not changed within the mental health field. White mental health therapists working with black kids are nearly as dangerous as white police officers. I said that because racist white counselors are traumatized and can only express white supremacy ideology. They live in a racist society with one objective and that's forcing the black race to see them as good (superior). Their main focus is teaching and preserving white supremacy. Now that makes them an ineffective therapist with black kids. The same as most white police officers. They want blacks to do as told and never challenge white authority, because it angers them in a psychological way. It's really reversed PTSD and it's real. OK, it's obvious these whites will never be effective. Because they believe in a dominant white culture, which is creating a stigma for failure within their own brain. They cannot process what's real, it's too confusing for them to face the truth.

Therefore, they force their lying culture upon black kids and it's hurting them. They cannot fix it; they can only make it worse. The same as most white police officers. They want blacks to do as told and never challenge white authority. They believe in a dominant white culture which creates a split personality, making it too confusing to follow. Brain malfunction displaying several personalities which confuses black kids. They hear and see differently. They are not capable of working with blacks. Therefore, they are only forcing their white culture upon black kids. In America most of the kids in state custody are black. While 99% of Medicaid and large white organizations are over seeing these black kids. The problem in most states is that whites seem to have privatized the health system. Therefore they have a type of ownership over our kids. It's another form of slavery. While the United States Government is steady sending money to these states and the kids are not receiving the help they need. They need blacks in charge.

I was talking to a white therapist the other day and he explained to me that he taught race diversity training. Now to me that's a joke. It's people who look like him are creating the race problem. He can't fix it, because he's a part of the problem. You can't train adults to not be a racist, but you can train small kids. That's what's happening within the mental health field. Whites are training whites to not be a racist and how to deal with race diversity (double crazy). They have some of the wrong people as therapists working with black kids, so the kids are trapped. That problem needs to be addressed. Because keeping our kids enslaved by the health care system is going unnoticed. Oh, I almost forgot Barack Obama. That judge up in Minneapolis Minnesota quoted him as saying something stupid. In reference to the killing of Daunte Wright, and it's a shame. I think she based her decision around that stupid statement. Maybe she's hearing something that we don't, or we're not listening close enough. Sounds like she was saying Barack Obama would not judge her decision as being wrong. I truly hope Barack Obama is not tripping that hard. But she said it for a reason. That shooting could have been avoided. But she had to show that white females needed to be in charge of black kids. The same as the white male. It's another delusion (insanity).

Their attitude needs to change, and no one should be able to privatize the health system. They get away with it because the government does not put stipulation on how the money is distributed towards black therapists who need to be the ones seeing the black kids. The stipulation should direct certain monies to black therapists to work with inner city kids, people they know. Otherwise, progress will not be made for black kids within the system. It's just a continuation of the players within the circus.

There was an interview that stayed with me. I was about thirteen years old when I saw a certain television interview. I remember it well, because it was so blizzard and challenging. The person being interviewed happens to be a United States Senator (Barry Goldwater). I would consider him to be an everyday white American. The question came up, "If you could change anything you have done, what would it be?". His answer startled me. He stated that he wouldn't change a thing, which is creepy and unacceptable. I thought to myself there has to be something consequential in this man's life that he wishes he hadn't done or should have done. I was eager to learn, but his answer left me struggling for years trying to process how in the world can anyone become so arrogant (egotistical). It took me years to figure out the message he was sending. But I believe at the time it was directly meant to encourage white males to never be remorseful. He was saying that white people are God on earth. Therefore, anything they do has to be acceptable because whites are perfect people. So, by his philosophy, slavery was a perfect, discrimination towards blacks was perfect, lynching, starving black kids was all perfect acts. He was saying there is nothing to fix, and that all whites should feel good about what they have and are doing to blacks. It's not wrong (no remorse).

Also raping black women and children was acceptable and perfectly patriotic. Along with mass incarceration and housing discrimination. Because white people are never wrong and their history is perfect. All a misconception of reality. All the uproar about Ukraine. Now, the atrocities that I just mentioned happened right here in America not long ago. But whites do not consider slavery and the abuse thrusted upon blacks as being wrong; they say it's what God wanted: meaning they are the one and only god.

Therefore, they do not want to do reparation for slavery because of their garbage mind set. We are perfect people and cannot do wrong. God on earth. So, the white people in Washington DC can spend blacks' money the way they choose. Rebuilding Europe again to look extremely nice. Yes, they are making plans to rebuild Ukraine and not reparation for slavery. Yeah, it's strange to hear white people talking about sending all the aid that Ukraine needs. Sending black taxpayers money to do all these things for Ukraine without doing reparation for slavery is insane. God is speaking to me to say to the people of America, do reparation for slavery.

America is only committed to European Countries because of white supremacy. They must keep all white nations looking perfect to maintain white supremacy. I say now is the time to do reparation for slavery. America needs to repent. This administration can stop trying to sell Ukraine the same as

George Bush sold Iraq. Because you should be concentrating on America's atrocities. So, you're actually not sincere. Other nations are bad, but never America, while America has done the worse. We have Haiti right off our shores and we won't lift a finger helping but we will rebuild white countries.

Yet and still white philosophy is always the same we're perfect people and do not need critical race theory. It's all madness, and people are out of control. Whites needed to learn how to unstop their mental blockage. In Retrospect blacks have to give insight to white people. Because odds are another white person may be trapped with institutional racism. The country has become educated on so many fronts. Therefore, any so-called "Making America Great Again '' is unscrupulous and does not take into account accumulated knowledge. There is nothing great in the past for America, only shame. So, that scenario was stupid to suggest from the beginning unless blacks don't count. Let's go back in time anyway to when white immigrants flocked to America. Upon arrival they were all forced to pledge their allegiance to white skin.

Suppress and punish blacks, even though they were white they still had to prove themselves worthy of being called a white America. The first thing they had to prove was their hatred towards blacks by inflicting all the damage possible. The second thing was to discriminate against blacks. After passing those tests they were considered acceptable white Americans. It was explicit institutionalized racism. Essentially designed to put whites ahead of blacks.

Something that cannot be hidden anymore. A large proportion of blacks have been left out of the American dream. Not because of not putting forth effort, but because of systemic racism. So, when I heard Joe Biden on National Television say it was the black parent's fault for black failure. Now this was conversely racist ideology. Wow, Joe sounded more like a plantation owner than anything else.

Another thing overlooked was that some Indian tribes owned black slaves as well. I guess it's fair to say that black people have been caught up in a hell hole by all other races in America. Also keep in mind that Joe Biden was extremely unpleasant and distasteful expressing his feelings about reparation for blacks as well, very nasty. I thought to myself this is not a man to lead America in this day and age. He's saying whites should take no blame in that statement. It sounded like Joe Biden was justifying white supremacy.

That's weird and extremely polarizing for blacks. I guess he forgot about slavery, and separate but equal. Blacks never got anything out of that deal. Never have they had a fair chance. Plus, overlooked blacks being terrorized by white police officers on a continual basis. That's the main thing racist people overlook; it's the damage they inflicted on blacks. Let's look at the damage. Alright, America must understand that psychological damage was done. We have Dissociative Disorders, Anxiety Disorders and a thing called PTSD which runs rapidly within the black communities. However, I do feel that Joe Biden has separated himself from the abuse of blacks and is now leading the people to a true promised land.

I was reading an article a while back and it struck me how ignorant some people are in America in reference to Institutionalized racism. Let's look at sharecropping. The question one should ask, is, was sharecropping one of the main evil tools used by whites to hold blacks back for nearly one hundred years after slavery. Alright, let's explore the depths of sharecropping and expose some of its rot that's still sticking. Blacks worked the land nearly as hard as slaves sharecropping, but yet and still they always ended up owing money. The boss-man capitalized on all the earnings. Blacks only received pennies, not enough to live off of, and never could get ahead. They couldn't get loans or move away. If they wanted to leave to better themselves, they had to run away. The slave tactics are still in place. Which usually meant jail or death. Now this went on close to one hundred years after slavery. Blacks were underpaid, discriminated against and kept in poor living conditions, and it was the law of the land. They were trapped.

Now I said all of that to say this. The article talked about a white lady elaborating on how her family came to America and worked hard to get ahead. She compared her family to a black family and stated that she did not believe in reparation for slavery which is stupidity at its highest level. I assume she wasn't aware of all the obstacles in the path of blacks. They have never had a fair chance. What this lady didn't understand was that the country her family came to was actually built by blacks with slave labor. America became rich on the backs of blacks. They worked twice as hard as her family, I'm sure she wasn't aware. In fact, they worked for three hundred and fifty years, sharecropping could fall under slavery. Because they still didn't pay blacks. Blacks never got their share. America became super rich, laying the foundation for wealth by cheating and abusing black people. Whites cannot compare themselves to blacks; it's a sign of ignorance. The nation has always been designed for whites to get ahead. So, REPARATION payout is the only thing that's going to equalize the wealth gap. We should embrace it and stop playing around, because there would be no powerful America without slave labor.

STOLEN COUNTRIES

Let's look at the countries that were stolen by the white man. Now all of this land stealing started within the last four or five hundred years, actually, by the black kings of Europe. But it got out of hand when white peasants in Europe saw a chance to own land. They went crazy after land. They built up forces and started resisting the black kings of Europe. Afterwards they left the owners of the land poor, just the way they always lived. Now, the countries involved are The United States of America, Australia, New Zealand, Canada, South Africa and a long list of Islands. All stolen land. But wait, let's put the entire continent of Africa as stolen. Because of the stolen goods and the suppression of trade. Plus, the isolation from the rest of the world as far as drawing business and large corporate companies to Africa. European countries have destroyed the entire continent of Africa. Because America and Europe have stopped other countries from trading with Africa, except for Russia and China and all they do is abuse the trade.

America doesn't do any trading with Africa. Why haven't we seen anything made in Africa, in America? It's crazy. America supports Europe in suppressing Africa. Yes, America is the one responsible for Africa being poor. After all the stealing and abuse of Africa the Europeans and American whites are still making themselves the victim, which is completely wrong. Just pay up, it's the only way to balance the world. Otherwise, it's going to tilt in the wrong direction soon. As for American whites they actually owe black people for more than three hundred years of work without pay. It's also embarrassing to see white people in Britain calling themselves a king or queen ruling over black countries. It's so sickening and below stupidity. It must stop now.

EVANGELICAL

Well, I'm going to tell you something that I know to be true. All people on earth during the time of Jesus birth were black. Except for a few isolated albinos (Caucasians) and at the time they were not strong enough to make a mark within the world. In fact, they were not recognized as being fully human. The huge mix-up is that a lot of white so call evangelicals are saying that Donald Trump is Christlike (Jesus). Well, my first question is how many people can be Jesus Christ? Second, how do you identify Jesus Christ, and third, how did Jesus carry himself? Alright, let's be honest for once. Now, hopefully all Christians know about the synoptic Gospels. Go there and read them. You'll know right away that Donald Trump and the entire Republican Party are not associated with Jesus, it's a self-serving organization. Designed to preserve white power, period. Their religion is 100% called Buddhism, and it is nowhere near Christianity. First of all, Jesus is a black man. Please get it right. Now Jesus never talked to a white person, while he was on earth. Because none lived in the holy land unless they were slaves. All those people were black and so was all the other races of people. To be factual about the Holy Land, Africa and Africa alone is considered the holy land. Because Christianity was 99% worshiped in Africa during this time, and most of the Middle East used to be considered parts of Africa. Israel is in Africa and I'm 100% sure of that. The mix up came with another white lie. The last questions are, can white evangelicals learn and are they interested in learning? Because Jesus is black and it's sinful to masquerade him as any other race (demonic).

Well, I recently had death in the family and went North for the funeral to Chicago and Wisconsin. I got to see my wonderful family, super cool. Along with old friends from the past talking the talk and walking the walk. God spoke to me in Chicago about writing and teaching people on the seriousness of the fabrications involved the History in America. I found that 99% of Americans have never learned history. They have been told a bunch of garbage. Especially from the Ivy League schools, which are all fictitious and designed to make the black man look and feel inferior. There were never any intentions of blacks being admitted. Now, a lot of white Americans are still fixated on holding blacks back especially in Washington DC. But other races are increasing these days becoming Americans. So, it's too confusing nowadays following the republican party, their trend is increasing the hate and the selling of fake white Jesus. Both totally unnecessary, because we know better.

It's time for blacks to finally get the things they have been denied for centuries. It has to be fixed now. They need to catch up. It's sort of weird for some whites to say, look at your condition black folks. I can see that you are a loser. But, that's a bad philosophy and not true. In fact, it's insane, because 90% of whites have always been the ones getting free things in America, plus they have always been stopping the progress of blacks. The evangelical thinks that they must rule over blacks and believe it's God's will. It's crazy to think such a thing is true. When God's own son was black. It's not Christlike. America is at a crossroad for blacks these days. However, the Republican Party and some Democrats are struggling trying to stop progress, which is reparation for slavery, and rectifies the dirty deeds thrusted upon poor black people. It's 100% not Christlike, but is a 100% continuation of evil, still lying about God. In America if you can prove that someone or something injured you, it's a payday. Well, it's obvious and a prevalent thing in America that blacks have been damaged for centuries through insane abuse, brutally tortured and it continues to this very day, physically and mentally. Mainly done by so called Evangelical Christian. No Christian would be a part of that mess. Oh, Christians were the ones who did the lynching of blacks.

Only a reparation settlement is the answer to equality. I'm the true prophet, by the will of God. I understand the Scriptures well, about the lady touching Jesus' garment. She came from behind Jesus in the crowd and touched his garment. Jesus immediately turned to his disciples and asked the question who touched me. No one answered, everyone denied touching him, but Jesus stated that someone had deliberately touched him because he felt the power go out of him. That Scripture has taught me many things about Jesus and how the Holy Spirit works. It's still teaching me how to understand the power of Jesus. I can somewhat relate to what Jesus said. I feel America, because every time I write and post, I feel power going out of me and sometimes it takes days to recover.

Okay, let me update you on some of the things I'm working on resolving. All known written knowledge was written and kept in Egypt and a few other Africa Countries. The world's only libraries. Now Egypt and all of Africa was filled with black people and all the writings in the bible were done by black people. They were educated and very rich. In fact, Africa was the richest continent in the world. Now, when the Romans came and conquered Egypt, they took the library back to Rome. But, keep in mind the Romans were black people as well.

It was the barbarian Germans who conquered the Romans and took away the library along with Jews to teach them. Because they couldn't read and write, so stealing people wasn't a problem. The truth is black Jews taught the world how to be civilized. It wasn't white people, none were around. Plus, the small groups of albinos who were around were isolated and couldn't read and write. After a few centuries the barbarians Germans had gathered all the knowledge from every library in Africa. Here is the kicker, they kept that knowledge away from the rest of the world for several centuries, coming to believe they were the smart ones. But, black Jews in Africa knew how to read and write so they rewritten most of what was taken. But never all. Jews also brought civilization to Asian people. Yeah, it's the black people that some Americans hate, are the ones who taught them.

It makes one wonder why whites go through so much trouble trying to make blacks look dumb and stupid. I'm positive this is the reason. They know and it's now a game of manipulation.

This game has gotten out of hand. No white male President whether they're Republican or Democrat can ever fix America. It's impossible, because it's a part of his everyday life which is systematic racism. White males can only do a little, while we need change, reparation now. It's important for Americans to SEE change through color in leadership. Also, put a stop to the recycling of wealth and power back to the same whites. The white male only wants things to basically remain the same, keep him in power, and only a few selected white females can get the job done, because some are caught up as well. Otherwise, it's just another stressful recycled mess.

I'm a therapist that understands the risk of actually doing therapy with dangerous clients. To make good progress one must enter into their world mentally. I'm not sure all therapists should go deep into their inner thoughts though, because it can become sort of tricky, you have to know how to get out. Remember "Silence of The Lamb", Hannibal Lecter, well he went in and couldn't get out. America is at its turning point and should ask the question. How does one navigate safely through such lawlessness, treachery and ruthlessness? It's obvious one must sell their soul to the Devil. In order to keep following a trend of lies and deceit. The participation is such a mockery, because it's uncivilized behavior. It has done tremendous damage to the group that you least expect. It's Donald Trump followers who have entrench themselves into fabrication like never before seen. How can they face God with a continuation of bad behavior? Because Jesus was not a thug, but their behavior is thuggish. This group is suffering from several diagnoses. Schizophrenia is one, now, there is no returning to the norm, because normalization is rationalizing and using common sense. To them common sense is the enemy, because it requires change. You see people who suffer from schizophrenia are on a mission to prove, they are right about whatever, common sense has changed to nonsense. Their acts can demoralize a civilized nation. Destroying intelligence and replacing it with moron characteristics (outlaws). Meaning that right is wrong and wrong is right. Characteristics of schizophrenia. Donald Trump is now a felon. But even felons get a pass with this group (anything goes).

Yes, the Obama Administration went far left. Maybe a little too far and fast for a lot of evangelicals. I know how you feel. In fact, I know Donald Trump's base better than he does. But how many people can afford an attorney like Daniel Webster, the one who argued a case against the Devil to return a man's soul. Remember him. Daniel was one of a kind. You know it takes a lot of nerve to take the devil to court. I think Daniel Webster's capabilities are being sorted out again except this time he's arguing the case on behalf of the devil. One thing I know for sure and that's God is not impressed with liars, in fact lying is an abomination against God. But in the schizophrenia world everything is make believe, so you create your own world. It has nothing to do with reality. In fact reality is the enemy.

The Scriptures say "Jesus Christ said that He is the Way, the Truth, and the Life". If Christ is Truth, then lying is moving away from Him. Being honest is about following in God footsteps, because God cannot lie. The bible also states that God despises most of all, a hypocrite. So, a hypocrite in layman terms are people who pretend to be something that they are not (fake). It goes deeper, these so call Christian also have a fictitious religious belief system that's filled with lies and dishonesty, which makes them a deceitful person. They only seeking self-recognition, to make a long story short, they are evil doers. They desire and seek public approval and it's never the approval of Jesus.

One must remember that hypocrites are not decent people, their mission is to plant deceit and create total chaos. Leading people astray, doing the devil's work. So, the thing is to clear your minds and help God's people, not destroy them. Here's our song "Against the Wind - Bob Seger & The Silver Bullet Band".

Donald Trump is dysfunctional along with his band of hoods (Evangelicals). Now listening to him makes a lot of Americans dysfunctional, because a lot of them are calling themselves Christian. But following him they have to give up Christianity. They forget that the bible says how can two walk together, unless they agree. Donald Trump is not a Christian, and the Republican Party these days have no affiliation with the character of Jesus Christ. They are whole heart and soul devoted to Donald Trump. It's demonic and crazy but for some strange reason people without Jesus are attracted to bizarre behavior.

Insanity is real and anyone who agrees with insanity needs a little help, maybe a lot. People using people to do their dirty work, it's a shame. God is not pleased. I have information that some of you just might find interesting as for the Republican Party nowadays. It has been proven that the Republican party is displaying behaviors from the past, even before the civil war.

They are disrespecting black people by making every attempt to take away their voting rights. Including citizenship, because they feel that these deviant acts will create more power for the white race. Its slogan is making America great again.

Meaning putting blacks and women back in their place. Now this is going back into time before the civil war. When whites in the southern states were like a roaring lion. Wild and uncivilized.

I can remember as a young kid just setting and listening to old men telling jokes. They were very articulate and hilarious. It was usually under my special shade tree molly. Most of the time I was the only kid there. But they all seem happy to see me. I guess because my dad and granddaddy were usually among the pack. I knew they all loved me and they knew I loved them. I cherished the times I spent with them. They gave me something unparalleled and unassuming with no direct advice, it was always anyway the wind blows. You had to figure it out for yourself. It was sort of like Jesus teaching his disciples. Jesus spoke in parables. They taught me lessons about life mostly through comedy or parables, it was never direct. I was in class alright and they were the teachers, yup, among the best in the world.

Anyway, I said that to say this. The Donald Trump trials that's taking place in the United States these days reminded me of one of the jokes one of the old men shared under my shade tree Molly. I think it was funny. Here's what he said, all the black people living on the white man's plantation were working in the lowland and it started pouring down raining and they were soaked and wet. So, they ran to the white Bossman and explained. It's raining so hard down there until we can't see our hands right in front of our face and we only have one raincoat. What are we going to do? The Bossman shouted get back down there and put it on the mule. I'm beginning to suspect a mule is more important than black people with today's decisions of the Supreme Court. By the way the Supreme Court is holding up the trials of Donald Trump. In each case there are black court officials in charge of the trial. The Supreme Court is operating these days just like that phrase, put it on the mule. It's using the same trend of thought. Degrading black people, because it's the right thing to do to blacks in charge (ignore them). A racist and rotten philosophy that has operated in America. Makes one wonder. What is making America great again. It sounds insane.

Alright, let's get to my little friend, Ron DeSantis, the governor of Florida. AKA "shorty". This guy is emotionally disturbed and has serious emotional damaged. He has the disease of racism and fascism and blaming it on God. Time has changed too much for his philosophy. He doesn't understand that this bad trip (slavery) never should have taken place in the first place. Now he's doing okay with the old people in Florida. But America isn't controlled by old people like Florida. Ron DeSantis has a loud nasty mouth plus he's stupid. This governor (Mr. Clown) says he's doing something for God. No, it's just his schizophrenia over powering him along with evangelicals. They are actually too dumb to recognize the spirit. Now so-called white people must understand that black people are done with their nasty ways. We will not return to the flit of the Republican Party's old ego trip.

Time to change, you have taken an Insane path. I know what you are doing. You're trying to regain the family members you lost after the civil war, your black families. Okay. But what you are missing and not able to process is a lot of black people are better educated than whites these days. It's very difficult to make a fool out of an educated person. So, in reality whites look like developmentally disable people. Banning books and saying slavery was a good thing (unconceivable). So, they should learn the things they have been running away from, all their lives, which is common sense. Ron can be as cruel as Hitler. Now since he's out of the president's race, he's lost for good, into the neverlands. He has a small mind.

Florida doesn't need a messy man as such, anymore. It's like he's on some type of drug. You know growing up in Mississippi, it seemed that there was always someone in Someone's family that either chewed tobacco or dipped snuff. I tried them both and they both failed me. The tobacco made me so sick, all I could do was crawl, and the snuff made me walk sideways. They both pulled me down. You know when things aren't good, you separate yourself, because bad things only pull you down further and further. Until you lose.

Alright, let's get into something that I really want to share, and it's about love. First of all, you can never get rid of love, once you have used it. Because, when a person falls in love with someone, they can never take it back. Because it correlates with God, giving you a gift. He never takes it back. You may backslide, even get a divorce, maybe start dating someone else. It doesn't matter. LOVE LAST FOREVER, IT NEVER DIES. Now the Scripture says that God is love. People, that's a hint about the Image, God created us in. I'm positive.

You know, God can make a rock rise up and rule the world, if necessary. Do you understand me? Because it's vitally Important that you do. About 99% of the people in this world have no idea how big God is. He's not about wealth, neither is he about power. God is love.

Learn people, that you can never escape your past love life. The sooner you learn this, the closer you get to God. There, I gave you one of my secrets, HAPPY NEW YEAR. Oh, one other thing, that's so real, I got your Black

Panther "Wakanda Forever kingdom", and it's all in my Image. Because I rule that Kingdom. Yeah, and here's our song "James Brown – The Boss

I know tragic and tragedy is baffling, and essentially brings about pain and suffering. But for a lot of people, it is through ignorance and reprehensible acts against nature, whereas People become their own God and involve themselves in heinous acts against humanity (monstrous). Like over running the Capital being violent. They either don't know the Scriptures or simply forget. But there is something called undefinable love, which is known as the blood of Jesus that emerges and takes some of us to a higher level.

There is no violence nor disobedience if you are concentrating on the New Testament, instead of the Old Testament, because we are no longer under the old law. The New Testament teaches that the love of Jesus conquers all misbehavior. You see pain and suffering hurts, but it teaches us how God is long suffering (hidden knowledge).

One can only achieve greatness, if they come to grips with their own suffering. You don't automatically have God's blessings. You have to earn it every day of your life. If you are following someone or something that's not Jesus. You are no longer saved. No matter what you are telling yourself.

It's all about being still and letting God be God. Because God loves all people. Jesus spoke of suffering. He asked His disciples if they would be able to drink from his cup, meaning suffering. I'm positive that suffering is the main fruit of the Spirit. Because, I know what it feels like and what it did for me. It gets your undivided attention. Now, when one becomes aware it alleviates the ominous impressions of future worries. Abraham Lincoln knew blacks needed land and payments, 40 acres and a mule. Kamala Harris also recognizes the Importance of finishing Lincoln's work. That is the only way Abraham Lincoln will rest in peace. We owe him that as patriotic Americans. So, Kamala, let's finish Lincoln's dream. You are the only one bad enough to do it. We both know that an act like that will settle this dangerous trend of hate. You must stop keeping black's poor. God is with us. It's also expressed in the new commandment that Jesus left: Love one another. As I have loved you, so also you must love one another. By this all men will know that you are My disciples, if you love one another. Our song "The Staple Singers Love Me, Love Me, Love Me".

It's time to deal with Critical Race Theory. Starting with every President who owned slaves should not be talked about in our schools. It's too painful for black kids to discuss. Jesus didn't teach lies, neither did he omit the truth. Therefore, people trying to stop the truth from going forth are evil doers and are not followers of Jesus. People, these clown presidents should be stricken from all history school books. No one should be classified as good people who own slaves, because they were not good people. They are the worst role models ever, because of slavery. Stop referencing these Presidents, because it's a disgrace for our kids to hear their names mentioned. One other thing, they should never be mentioned in the top ten Presidential brackets. They were slave owners which automatically makes them psychopaths. All the raping, beating and extreme disrespect towards blacks. They can only be called maniacs, not Presidents. It's wrong for American kids to hear their names mentioned, especially in a classroom setting. Their names should be removed from all school books the same as the confederate statues were removed, because it's so sickening and demonic. We don't want to learn about slave owners. They were terrible people. It also gives black kids PTSD.

That's sending the wrong message to American kids, and it must STOP. Slave owners were very hateful people, along with the US Government and dirty state laws. One can only say that there were all Immature people in charge. In all actuality these Presidents were against humanity and a stain on mankind.

Now, there are also corn bread black people playing copycat behavior, which is an impediment to the progress of blacks. First let me explain what a corn bread black person means. To cut it short, it's a black person who wishes they were white. It's wired, because it creates a perilously veiled undeveloped personality and the person is left with a distorted reality. Also, when you take a real close look at these blacks, you will discover that they are the most indecisive group. They are constantly trying to be accepted by whites and behaviorally abandon blacks' style of living, and join people like Mitch McConnell, who is Mr. Confederate guy and that's all he has to offer. But most blacks are reluctant to accept the essential concepts of the American laws and lifestyle because it excluded blacks and they didn't have any say so in the plannings. So, they approach most things with skepticism, not to be drawn into a whop deceptive reality. Because not long ago a lot of black parents were teaching their kids to behave exactly as white kids, so they became superficial.

Those black parents failed to help establish their kid's individuality, which helps develop personalities. Therefore, perpetuating a reality of a lost cause, something that most white kids learn which is as confusing as Batman and Robin. It does not serve them well. It's unexplained behaviors that's holding white America families back, like OCD. Here's our song "Love Unlimited Orchestra - Satin Soul".

I learned from my parents that once you set your mind to do something, always finish the job. My sophomore year in high school. I decided I wanted to be on the football team. My weight was one hundred and five pounds, and I was at a tender age of fourteen. Yeah, I made the team. Now down there in Mississippi there was only one football team. It was known as the varsity, which usually consisted of juniors and seniors. Well, it's on my mind because I ran into several old friends in Mississippi two weeks ago at my brother's funeral. They were on that team, we sat and talked about the old days. One talked about how big I had become and that no one could stop me now. I'm nearly an old man, and he kept calling me 'SUPER NET'. Being a therapist, I was beginning to suspect something was wrong. Then he reminded me that my high school coach named me super net and that's what most of the players called me. I had completely forgotten about high school football. Let me tell you, it was a trip. I wore a size six shoe, but they gave me a size eight. I had a helmet that could turn around on my head and had shoulder pads that came down to my waist, with pants that a big fat belly-man could wear.

But I could play and I didn't care what I had on. However, it didn't take the coach long to fix me up. The scriptures say "For by the grace given me I say to every one of you: Do not think of yourself more highly than you ought, but rather think of yourself with sober judgment, in accordance with the faith God has distributed to each of us.

Another thing I always keep honey in my house. I think it reminds me of my dad. I remember a conversation we shared that changed my life for good. I thought I was open minded. Come to find out I wasn't. I may have been eight or nine years old. My daddy had three bee boxes and each one had large groups of bees, making honey. I can remember as a kid watching him get the honey from the boxes. Sometimes, he would get stung. My mother would always tell him to put on the bee gear, but on most occasions, he wouldn't wear anything.

He would just get the honey using a little smoke. Afterwards, I would always ask if he got stung. Each and every time he said yes.

I hated the bees for hurting my dad.

One day I told him I hate the bees for stinging you. He smiled and spoke these words "Oscar, do you ever feel sorry for the bees, because I'm taking their honey". I couldn't answer, because it was too much for me to process. I thought about it for about three weeks, and then one day out of the blue. I gave him an answer. Well, that's the only time in my life my father ever called me wise. Aww, but I paid it no mind. I think being open minded is an everyday practice. It has to stay fresh in your mind. If Jesus went around being deceitful and lying. We would not have anyone to emulate. Meaning there would be no Christianity. Alright Politics and Christianity are separate. Jesus mentions it. So stop, because you are beginning to look and sound like a fool. Your Christianity has turned into a gigantic cult. Here's our song "Luther Vandross - Dance with My Father"

Well, I want to talk about something that will help the lost Christians get back on track. There are several things' Evangelicals are overlooking involving the Gospels, especially the book of John. The Gospel of John Introduces us to the Holy Spirit. The Holy Spirit, is connected to the Father and the Son. But it has a different function. It makes Jesus divine. It also connects us to Christlikeness.

Christlikeness is the key. The ministry of the Holy Spirit is to glorify Christ. So, if you have a pastor or a spiritual leader in a group and they are not glorifying Christ. Then that's the problem of all the problems. Christians must teach and lead keeping in mind that everything should be focused on conduct geared toward displaying Christlikeness. When Jesus walked the earth, the disciples had Him to lead and give directions personally. Today's Christians are without Jesus in the flesh; however, they have the Holy Spirit inside of them acting as a guide. Reframing them from acting unseemly.

I think the problem with today's Evangelical Christians derives from not being able to separate themselves from the Old Testament. Whereas people didn't have the holy spirit during that time. Today they do, except I think they are not familiar with its usage.

Today, people are still unable to understand what Jesus taught, neither do they understand what the writings of the Bible are actually saying without having the Holy Spirit. Instead of the Holy Spirit working through Jesus in the flesh, Christians now have the Holy Spirit working in them directly. They become intensely involved in doing what is right, their focus in life is transferred from self to God through Jesus as they grow in the likeness of Christ.

The disciples knew the characteristic of Jesus, because they see him close up. So, after Jesus left, they came to find out that the Holy Spirit possessed the character of Jesus Christ. It taught them to be thankful, and obedient, to have self-denial, humility, and to surrender the things of this world. They realize that they couldn't do it without the holy Spirit leading and guiding them in all ways of righteousness. The Holy Spirit taught them the meaning of suffering, just as Jesus did, and to be patient and utilize its power to resist the evil one. The disciples understood that the power of the Holy Spirit came upon people when they believed and accepted that Jesus was the Savior of the world. Personally, I will not follow a person who doesn't have a testimony of getting saved. They must be able to describe it in detail, because it's something you will never forget.

The disciples were as most people of the world today, doing their best to be honest and good but without the power and wisdom necessary to avoid being carried away by their selfishness and own desires, they became disoriented, discouraged and ashamed, much like people today. Sin has control over people's lives if they do not have the Holy Spirit within them, they will follow anyone talking about what they want to hear. That was just as true during the time of the disciples as it is today. This sinful nature blinds people to God's wisdom and knowledge, but all things are possible through the Holy Spirit.

My biggest problem with Evangelicals today is that none of them have led Donald Trump to Christ, after all this time. He's still evil and they support his evilness. What happen to Christlikeness? God is not in his demeanor, and appearance means a lot. Evangelicals Christians are embarrassing because they have abandoned Christlikeness. Which is the most essential part of being a Christian.

FRANKLIN GRAHAM PUBLIC MORON STATS

Franklin Graham stated that blacks are not qualified to serve in Joe Biden's administration. He's delusional. That's weird and flat out dumb. Well, I don't walk hand and hand with his premise. Simply because I disagree with his delinquent hillbilly statements. He's insulting an entire race of black people with that statement. It's the same kind of talk that whites feed upon, that's racist. There is no place in America for this type of foolishness. It's so immature and childish. Let me update this guy on something. BRER RABBIT (Franklin Graham) blacks are more than qualified to run this country. The problem hasn't been blacks running the country but the opposite, whites. People it is people like this moron who is considered a demonic preacher, who spread hate, and has kept the ideas of white supremacy thriving throughout the America. Did he pray for Barack Obama? NO. So, hold your horses and learn T MODEL, because you're left behind, racism is getting old fashion. That kind of talking is gone with the wind. We don't do that anymore people, because it's a lack of intelligence. It needs to stop, it's a thing of the past. People get save and come to black Jesus. Because He's real and not made up. OK. Rise above it if you can, but understand the need to say nice things especially about black people. Jesus was black. People that hate blackness, really hate Jesus. People must realize that whites have pulled themselves down, wasting time trying to slow black Jesus down. It's embarrassing to see and hear these days that people are still not accepting Jesus as being black. I think all of us have had the game ran on us once or twice, by slickers. But for some of us it's hundreds of times (limbo). There is an old saying, game recognizes game, so shut it down players. That's only if you're intelligent enough.

Because it should be impossible to keep running the same game on the same people generations after generation. It seems like people should get tired of being the fool all the time. Usually, the person running the game ends up being alone, deserted. But we forgive people who tell the truth. When people confess things in the midst of a heated battle, they win our love. Here's our song "Haters Gonna Be Hatin'".

It sounds like Franklin Graham has been programed to think eating soup with a folk makes sense. If he is told to do so by Donald Trump. Then it becomes a religious ritual, along with a whole lot of other cult followers. They wouldn't think much about it, especially the Mega Republicans, because they are such an obedient group and have separated themselves from anyways associated with Christianity (reality). They are willing to accept anything, except following Jesus (Christlikeness). Jesus said if you hate your brother, you have committed murder. Aww, they overlook that one, because hate is their main thing. So, Graham would immediately start sucking the soup off the folk with no questions asked. But the rest of us would recognize that it's not the proper utensil for soup. Smart people would stop right away. Because, it looks like one is being making a fool out of themselves. I would say, I don't monkey around like this. I need a spoon and that's just using common sense.

The church is not trying to resolving the race problems. In fact, they are the one group that's encouraging and motivating the rest of the world to be racist. Here's a way to fix the problem with race. Ask all the questions about race that society is struggling with right now, before, they get accepted into any American college, and that goes for every student domestic and from abroad. Society must stop babysitting racist people. They mean to hurt people because of the color of their skin. Their philosophy is black is bad, even though Jesus was black. It should not be tolerated. Let's bring an end to it and put it into writing. Because they need to be identified. That's the only way to stop it. The same should go for any job one applies for in America. These are things that should be added on to applications; like Racism is wrong and we will not tolerate it, especially in high schools. So, let's start eradicating it once and for all. Ask the question, are you a racist? Do you dislike black people. That way the problematic people will be turned away. People will know that racism is not tolerated from the beginning. That will be a start at Making America Great.

CRIME

Now the enduring patterns of the republican party has always been tough on crime, along with the essential features white men rule not women. Listen to how they talk about crime. It's scary these days especially the recently laws, you know the ones created to torture women and children, it's the new abortions' laws designed to lock up little girls and women, which are now considered criminals. The strange thing about this new tough crime law is most American women and little girls don't understand exactly how men could ever own their bodies. Here is the main question with this dilemma. What kind of a man would want to do something like that to women and children? Answer: Only Satan and his angels and I'm 100% sure of that. It's the work of the Devil and it's called witchcraft.

Well, It's a new thing and it's just the beginning. It will never stop once it's starts. The Republican Party will have the opportunity to reopen concentration camps in America. Straight out of the Nazi playbook. The Nazi Party was a political organization that gangrened people and ruled through murderous, and totalitarian ways, strictly barbarian behavior. They do not care about certain groups of people just as the Republican Party has extreme hatred toward women, and believe in total domination of women. Look at it closely. You will see that the Republican Party is Identical to the Nazis Party and they will keep getting worse and worse until it's horrible. They are leading to the extermination of black people and women who do not follow their guidelines, 100% positive. They must be stopped.

Make the mistake and vote for them anywhere on the ticket, it will be like signing yourself over to majestic wolves who will eventually devolve you.

Better known as genocide. Alright. Just keep in mind that the Republican Party has criminalize abortion, so they can regain their property, which is considered women and blacks. They will never change their minds. They will keep coming until they achieve their goal which is genocide. Don't forget. You will be considered as criminals, even though you have never broken the law before. It's up to women and people of color to stop them. I'm 100% positive.

The Republican Paty has turned into a criminal enterprise. Donald Trump their President is now a felon and will probably serve jail time. He's constantly breaking laws. He has cases outstanding against him; however, the Supreme Court has held up all of the cases, in hopes of him becoming president, so white supremacy can reign supreme. Their philosophy is their law and it was written to protect the white race, and some white women who have been as they put it, contaminated with race mixing. Because that is one of their main objectives. The white man's ego is too large to share anything. It's not only Donald Trump (Mack Daddy), but the Legislative and Judicial branch of government have joined with the Executive as well as the Supreme court. The only thing they are interested in these days is having a king. They don't believe in the law anymore (trials) that do not work in their favor. They seem to be under the impression that public opinion is the only thing that matters, not the law of the land. No trials for white males. Meaning the law is for women and blacks. They have no pity for these groups. They see them as public enemy number one, and it's on the same scale. Other minorities are included.

THE HISTORY OF AMERICA

I have written on the cause of The Civil War several times over the years. It appears that America wasn't paying close enough attention. So, we are now on the verge of maybe another Civil War. American History has not been explained well. Because the dynamics that really started The Civil War, was 100% the United States Supreme Court decision on March 6, 1857. I assure you it was The Dred Scott Case, which was about a runaway slave. The Supreme court voted 7-2 that African Americans could never become citizens in the United States. No matter what state they lived within. They also stated that blacks would always be slaves throughout the United States. So, confederate white people still do not consider black people to be free, and are still pushing the old slave law of the Supreme Court decision, before the civil war. So, that's what Donald Trump means, when he says that the race was stolen. Black votes should not count. So, it took a civil war to end that decision. But it may resurface in the supreme courts. It's a kangaroo court.

This stop the steal talk is all about black votes not being counted. Because they are not citizens. This ideology has created a group of modern-day traitors trying to overthrow the United States government. They are the ones who should not be citizens, because they do not respect the constitution.

These people are without a country. They have regressed back in time to a place before the civil war whereas barbarian behavior was accepted. They make threats and talk about blood all the time. Plus, they are still using the confederate flag and the Sasakwa. These flags have no country as well. We are really witnessing a group of traitors on the loose in America. They need to be stopped by using the law correctly.

Now, The Trump followers actually want black people and women to lose their citizenship and return to slavery conditions meaning blacks should not be able to vote, because of the Supreme Court's decision in 1857. The cause of the Civil War.

Alright people, it's time for another reality check which brings us to psychology, along with nonsensical arguments. Alright, let's look at it, for what it is, on one hand Sigmund Freud believed the unconscious mind mostly promotes incentives that control a person's social and moral behaviors. Meaning human connections are the main motivating drive for behavior (intimacy). On the other hand, Alfred Adler saw behavior altogether different. He explains that behavior starts formulating in childhood and manifests throughout life with feelings of inferiority, and the main point is for people to work towards is overcoming this inferiority by striving for superiority. Alder believed that this drive was the main force motivating human behavior, emotions and thoughts, working to overcome the inferiority complex.

Stay with me here. I agree with Adler on this subject, because competition would be closely connected to Adler's approach. In America we are consumed with being number one. Athletes practice and practice to get better than their competition. Their desire is to be number one, the best. Alright hold that thought, because we're painting this picture together and it's going to be a beautiful painting like the Mona Lesa. It's a painting of America as we grow and explore unexplored depths, forming a great cohesion making America whole. Let me say this off the bat, no one wants to be a loser. So, I think Adler had the right idea about growth towards overcoming inferiority. However, God has revealed to me the importance for all people to go through the phases of growth while trying to achieve superiority.

Most of us were taught by our parents as children to never cheat and always be honest, nice and respectful toward all people. Here's where the problem in America gets out of hand: 65% of white people never finish the process of growing out of the inferiority complex, because they never learn the fundamentals of how to treat people. They were taught blacks were inferior and to never respect them. So, here is where things fell apart for whites who were being raised to be good people but racist at the same time, which is conflicting and confusing for kids. They become unstable because it's contradicting and very difficult to process. So, parents force racism upon their kids. It is not something they learn except it's taught.

Now, it's impossible to do both, be good and bad. So, they must choose one or the other. But let me remind you that racism creates full blown schizophrenia, sociopathy behavior along with conduct disorder and antisocial behavior. All very serious diagnoses, which are the offspring of fascism. Creating an insane group of people. Alright, it's all about wrong teaching. There is no love in teaching racism, only hatred and it's Impossible to be a follower of Jesus Christ. Jesus taught love; never did he teach hate. To be totally honest no race is superior to another. It's manipulating and destroying young people's creativity by telling them creepy distorted lies about blacks. It's really teaching them their own inferiority complexities. We need to teach the truth about American History. The worst thing you can do to a child is teach them that they were born with superior genes. God didn't create that kind of a human being. What you are really doing is calling God a liar, and telling God that he did not create every race equal. Now, this kind of teaching entraps white kids' growth. So, it's impossible for them to reach superiority, they can only fake it, because of insufficient patterns of development. Their parent's mission was to brainwash their kids into believing they have already achieved superiority, without going through the phases, which brings us to cynical thinking and it's not good.

Now about 65% of white people are operating on false premises and are disingenuous in their behaviorisms and have stopped using common sense altogether. Maybe it's something they have never learned, fake Leave it to Beaver. All they do is give inflammatory speeches about total madness which expresses their inferiority complexities. They don't see anything wrong with their behavior because all they have learned are defense mechanisms, which includes lying, denying, cheating, stealing and abusing blacks. When you listen to whites who have suffered the most from this disease. You only hear propaganda and divisiveness. It's a never-ending fairy tale in their minds, making them immature. It's childish and it's like a two-year-old throwing a temper tantrum. All of their behaviors are geared toward being rulers over blacks.

It's as though America made them slaves and they have always been marginalized people in America using reverse psychology. I interpret their action as saying that they are incapable of stabilizing their behavior, because of the ambiguity of living among blacks, Incendiary and emphatically egregious. It's a hopeless case of immature people in control. Black kids shouldn't have to go through the lying and misleading history again. It doesn't make sense we already know you're a lying fake and has basically stolen everything. Plus. The lying and belittling of black Kids, gives them PTSD. All kids need to learn the truth about how rotten America has been toward blacks. So, we can do something about it. They can handle it and put it behind them once and for all, because kids are resilient. Here's a kicker how dumb can the people be in the state of Virginia. I can't believe a grown man just won the state of Virginia's Governorship. By simply stating something I write about in almost all my writings, start reading and learn people.

Critical Race Theory is not explained well. So, let me fill you in on what it's trying to say. Here we go. It's saying there is something wrong with the States and The United States Government laws. They are racist. Because of its laws and unfair treatment toward black people and that it needs to be fixed now. So, please don't come back with that Critical Race Theory mess anymore, unless you have an Intellectual disability. History is called history for a reason. Meaning, it took place and must be documented.

You can't change History using witchcraft. Stop living in fantasy land. It will never serve you well. History has a way of repeating itself. Maybe not what people had in mind. Americans are not stupid enough to put a donkey in the Kentucky Derby and expect him to win. Some of us are intelligent people with sound minds and we are capable of making sound judgment calls.

Well, looking at the people of Virginia decision makings, it's a true manifestation that solidifies pure ignorance with no Modern day starting points. They are saying slavery didn't take place in America, an example of ignorance trying to replace intelligence with moron behavior. An extraordinary polarization of America, first hand. Determining to brainwash all Americans. Alright, here's an old Indian Proverb "The White Man Speaks with a fork tongue". I tell you what, go try eating a bowl of soup with a fork. When I look at the white males and their actions. It's actual a reenactment of the slave master expressing his dominance over anyone that's not a white male. This governor is a slap in the face toward women and they fell for it. His aim was to punk out a whole race of black people. Because if you don't let Donald Trump and the white males control you. YOU'RE NOTHING. That's American with the drum major instinct. It's a macho thing, that's out of control and it's also carrying a stigma that says get in line white folks. The stereotype, no blacks should count, and all whites should think alike.

The Old Testament doesn't teach women how to be holy, but the New Testament does. So, men leave women alone. Remember Paul said when I'm in Rome I act as the Romans. Alright, when you're in America, learn to act as Americans. Because America is truly different from the rest of the world. It's all my show, no matter what party you are affiliated with, because God sent me. So, I have to tell you the truth. I'm an advocate of women. Nancy Pelosi is a great warrior, but watching Nancy Pelosi make illegitimate excuses to not impeach Donald Trump was disturbing, delusional and weird. Because he has done enough out in the open to be impeached. What Nancy was doing is just as bad as Donald, 100% self-interest and has abandoned the constitution altogether. America is faced with two Narcissistic leaders and it's obscure to think that either can govern.

It's like these guys are coming out of the fifties lost in time. Whereas women were passive toward a dominant white male during that time, poor personification. Nancy Pelosi is missing the whole point. It's all about facing off with a dominant white male and this is your opportunity. As a female, you have to prove to America that you can do it. Passiveness doesn't work. You have to stand and fight. It's your chance to show that you can go toe to toe with the dominant white male. Because believe it or not, most American men and women think women are afraid to face off with a dominant white male.

Everyone is watching you run away, Nancy. That looks cowardly. Judging by America standards no woman is able to lead as a President. Women are too weak to lead in America, sadly to say. On the one hand it appears that it's literally not sustainable for women. On the second-hand Donald brings something new to the stage that no previous administration was able to handle. He's the best con artist in the world. Here's our song, " I'll Take You There - Staple Singers".

I'm positive that It's wrong to raise girls to think it's alright to be submissive to any male, because it suppresses her Intrinsic qualities. That's why she procrastinates most things and still follows polarizing male figures like pimp daddy and nut balling cool. Subordination is not a role for American women, so denounce it.

It's really witchcraft and women must rise above it because there is nothing in it for her. Men and women are equal, so ladies vote together distinctively. There is no party line for a woman, you're an outcast. The Republican Party only wants to use you. Period. Yeah, subordination actually makes women indecisive about being misunderstood, leading some women to believe the Republican Party is good, while most of its intentions are build around controlling white women. So, let me update you. Women used to be second class citizens and it was terrible then and always a struggle. But since Roe v Wade women are now third or maybe fourth class. It appears that pimping is back. Mack Daddy on the scene. Women almost have no rights, merely existing. But wait, hold your horses. I see women as the world's last hope. Men need you, so, now is the time ladies. Reach out and touch the world and get the pimps out of your head. They don't love you enough. Rise up like a Pokémon. You know who the people are that's hurting you. So, make up your mind and bring an end to all this witchcraft. It's women votes that can do it, especially white women.

Therefore, there's no need for women to get back to second class, skip witchcraft and go straight to first, because you should be able to see the flaws now. Stick together like peas in a pot forget about race, it's a trap. The race card is only for white male dominance. They are making a fool out of you. You will never have equal rights unless you take them. Be wise enough to understand that the bible and customs change with time. That means subordination is no longer affective. So, let's culminate together ladies. I'm the poster boy for the me-too movement. Here's our reflection point. Now, I have been carrying you for the longest. Stand up for yourself, once. I would love to see it. Please don't let men take you back into the kitchen.

They are trying to neutralize women, so look out. Women rule because there's more of you, so start acting like it and stick together. Because men do and it's called dominating a foolish woman. White males will keep making a fool out of you. Because they are macho and believe they are the only people that matter in America. They feel that they are the true rulers of America and no one should be equal to them. That's why insane Donald Trump is so popular. You must not let them get away with that philosophy. It's not Christ-like. You have been fooled by the church. Now they are devil worshippers.

I was cooking a big meal last weekend, it unwinds me. The kind of meal that takes three to four hours to finish. So, I grabbed an old movie, put it on without paying any attention to what it was. I like watching old movie, but what I don't like is how blacks were portrayed to look so stupid. But besides that, I love watching old movies. It's just an old habit of mine. Putting on an old movie while cooking. Anyway, this movie was about James Stewart starring in "IT'S A WONDERFUL LIFE". Now, I usually watch such a movie during Christmas time. I put on this particular movie by mistake. However, I never watch movies while cooking, I only listen. It affects you, sort of like reading a book. If you have never done it before you may struggle. Because it's hard to do.

The movie comes on and the main character is trying to commit suicide. All of a certain an angel appears and explain to him that he shouldn't do that. Then the character stated that "he wishes he had never been born". So, the angel granted his wish. Here comes the tricky part. This one person distinctively made a world of difference to that little city. So, the angel took him back and showed him what the city would look like without him. It wasn't a pretty sight.

Afterwards, he begins to appreciate the small things that made him a good person. Here's what I have to say tonight. I started thinking about us and how easy it was and is for us to hear one another. It crossed my mind, what if we were never born. The thoughts sent me back to reading Hidden Knowledge, a book I wrote. You know dealing with saving Obamacare, not only was I after John McCain, but also Susan Collins and Lisa Ann Murkowski as well. **I had to save Obamacare to save America.**

Alright, let me tell you a marvelous story about a man who fell asleep for a continuous stretch of years. Some of you may know the story of Rip Van Winkle but to those of you who are not aware of Old Rip, let me update you. Well, it's all about a guy who falls asleep in the Catskill Mountains and the poor guy awakes twenty years later and the world has changed in so many ways. It was unprecedented, strange and weird. Simply because twenty years had passed and the people's appearance along with their thinking had changed. It's a story that's unfathomable for most people. Alright, I have to make a confession before I go any further. Old Rip is one of those stories that made my imagination run wild and my feelings got deeply involved. Yes, I have always felt sorry for Rip Van Winkle because I'm not sure if he ever recovered. Yet and still it's a great story. However, I often wondered if he dreamed or not. I think he did.

Now, let's get into this Roe v Wade. Oh, first let me explain the sleeping giant is American White Women. Roe v Wade has awakened her and she can no longer wander aimlessly. If she wants to survive. I was beginning to think it would never happen during these times. Yet, I have been writing about her for years. I have often reminded white males that she is his greatest threat. I don't think he knows, but then again, maybe he does. Now it's interesting again. Will she save herself or continue in the path of destruction? I can truly say that America is the most interesting country in the world and she is ever changing, mainly because of women.

Who's the biggest fool? Well, that's not a mystery in America these days, it's white women and they are now in a struggle to be free and it's embarrassing. It's a shame she hasn't learned, yet. The struggle is the same as in the fifties and sixties, when blacks struggled seeking equal rights. Black men and white women are both closely tied together and cannot be divided. The sooner they learn that part, the stronger the force becomes between the two, and they will be unstoppable. The difference is blacks knew who the oppressor was, whereas she does not fully understand who's doing the oppressing. It's 100% the entire Republican Party and I mean all. If you are different, change the name of your party, along with your behavior. There are no good Republicans, because they are against blacks and white women. I know, just look at the creepy people they vote into office. They are out to take away blacks and white women rights at all cost. These are the people who put the abortion laws in place, and they are not done yet. They stole blacks voting rights and gerrymandering is legal now days. They are like broken toys a group of misfits. You don't believe me; watch how they vote. So, be careful. Remember. that a person who votes against themselves has a serious mental illness.

No Republican male should win anything and that's on every ticket on all levels. Because he brings the same thing to the table that has been going on for centuries and that's nothing. They are brazening and not trying to change, just another macho bully with a job description. Never let a black man or woman lead in America in their party. They try to prevent that. They believe blacks are blue collar works and women belongs in the kitchen. If they do get an important position, they find a way to take the power away at all cost. Yes, that philosophy should stop. But, you have to vote to stop it. Yet, it's the same play they keep running. So, brace yourself and hold your ground together. Now, don't get played again, it's time to take ground, because you're in charge of you, so vote together. Now, any vote for Republicans is a flat out vote for the devil. Because they are thuggish and don't mean women any good. It's the party that makes everyone look stupid who disagrees with them, one mind set. That's very old fashioned and close minded. They are hiding behind the religion of the Old Testament and are not showing any Christlikeness. Because they don't know Jesus. They are evil doers that love to follow the devil in the name of the lord. Hypocrites.

What kind of people will do women as such. It could only be witchcraft and it's 100% evil. It's the party of garbage minds and it stinks. The smell only gets worse day after day. It's one thing after another and Jesus is nowhere to be found, that's sad.

Look out ladies, they want concentration camps for women. It's the resurrection of the Nazis. I'm positive. Where else could they detain so many women? There is one last hope, play your poker hand and it's a winner. I'm sure you're tired of being the fool. The shoe may fit someone else, let them try it on. It's the white woman and black man's world, nowadays. Send the white man on an expedition looking for bigfoot. That's something he may love to do.

WEAPONS OF WAR

I think most of us have lost a family member or friend. It's painful and we experience different symptoms, but we all go through things physically, emotionally and behaviorally. Support is a beautiful thing. We need to take away the AR-15. It's a monster without a conscience and I still see it in my sleep. Another thing that's troubling is racism and fascism. People with this diagnosis are the ones who need counseling. Once a person has shown signs of being affected with this diagnosis. They are dangerous and should immediately be put into counseling. It's a sickness that's cannot be controlled and these people need to be on medication. It's a high percentage of the white race. They are the cause of the spreading of hate, which is the engine that's engineering the destruction. They need to stop except they can't, so we must establish a reforge safe haven to help eradicate their self-destructing trend of thought. So, not having racism as a diagnosis in the DSM- V is as dumb as having AR- 15's on our streets. It's a killer and it's legally Insane, and I'm 100% positive of that. We need to focus on eradicating fascism and racism first. Because that mind set is definitely what's keeping the AR- 15 on our streets. So, eradicating racism and fascism automatically gets rid of the weapons of war.

The nation needs counseling for these people because they have lost touch with reality. They are being taught to be mad people. Yet justifying it, as being righteous. Their whole teaching is about white supremacy based on made up old fashion stories, which are all lies. Design to make a fool out of the white race as well as the black. Just to carry on nonsense, that you are better than a black person. The thing is we are not enslaved people anymore. Black people are educated these days. So that stupid manipulation game looks so childish and yes, it looks like nearly a whole race of people are throwing a big temper tantrum. We need to focus more on this tragedy. It's really like a two-year-old kid saying let me have my way. Because of who I am. No, it's totally nonsense. Grow up people and do reparation for slavery and free yourself from bondage. Make America Great Again is simply saying, make America a barbarian country that's uncivilized. Because we are full of hate and that's all we have learned.

Who are they going to war with? The weapons are on the streets of America. Why? I think because it's a part of the race war planned, almost all whites own an AR-15, because it's their Jesus. They worship violence instead of Jesus. They want to kill black people. They are crazy with fictitious thoughts and are very dangerous people. They tell themselves the blacks are coming, and they can't stop the foolish thoughts. Now there is no black people really giving them a second thought. Because black do not dwell on violence. Whites should stop telling themselves that black people are out to get them. It has been all made up and passed on to you. It's called SCHIZOPHRENIA which is coming out of fear of the replacement theory. Just learn to live together in peace, people. We learn from our mistakes from the past. It's like growing up. Who wants to go back in the past and become a kid again? It will not be a pleasant experience because we're more mature.

The Make America Great Again slogan is petrifying, because it abandons knowledge. Why should we as a nation entertain thoughts that's tapping into insanity. Equality and education bring America one step closer to true greatness. Most of the past in America has been a group of ignorant people trying to lead without accumulative knowledge, not able to use common sense because of fear. That doesn't work today and it has never worked in the past. So, "Make America Great Again "is like saying, I love being a fool, so please help me look like a bigger fool.

Now, fox news is frightening to watch, because all they have is fear and they sell it as though the sky is falling. Especially Tucker Carl and Sean Hannity before changes were made. They were like the *One Flew Over the Cuckoo's Nest* novel. It was a movie. It's all about the behaviorisms of people in a psychiatric hospital. It was truly an insane person leading the insane. What made the movie so interesting is how hard their leader was working and yet they didn't accomplish anything. Except more trouble. Some of them recognized that they were insane. But their leader didn't, so they followed him and kept getting into more and more trouble. It was like the blind leading the blind. Because his reality was filled with the thoughts of schizophrenia. Meaning, nothing is real. They make up things as they go along.

Well, God allows us to make our own decisions which sometimes goes against His will, creating a stigma whereas God suffers. Now, we know that there are many intricate parts to The Civil Rights Movement. However, it is now an American movement on top of the Civil Rights Movement. We must do the right thing and get the voting rights bill passed. Sentiments for whites have to change for America to be great. The slave master's mentality is still operating in the mainstream, especially in congress. It's outdated. White supremacy is sick and stinks, rotten to the core. If you are associated with that mentality, you have failed in life, because there is no cure, you are trapped.

Oh, don't forget we will deal with reparation and I mean that. It's time and it must be dealt with now. You're trying to dance around it and that's a no-no. OK, all the house of representatives are doing now is precipitating hatred toward blacks by putting disgusting one sided bills on the floor and having the mindset to think it's a good enough bone to throw to blacks (HELL NO).

Richard Pryor said a long time ago that the white man needs a new fool. So, keep looking. There is an enigma here for most people, but the viable option is for the white race to thrive and steadily leave blacks further behind the connotation: we're too slick for blacks. Catch up because it's essentially important for whites to make race progress. The world is changing too fast to back track. It's crazy looking at this vaccine thing. It makes one wonder who's not civilized. People You're not who you think you are, please learn the truth, and take the chip off shoulder. Because it's paramount that people learn true history, and face it gallantly, so we can stop this maniac cycle of hate.

BLACKS

Black people in the state of Georgia at one point in time was the only place in America where as a black person was truly welcome and shown respect. Now, it changed over time, but it was the first natural American place where blacks felt safe. Georgia tried to avoid slavery. I know a lot of people figured it was in the north in places like New York. But you are wrong. Please Keep in mind that slavery was more prevalent in the north in places like New York, Massachusetts, and New Jersey more so than any other place in America. Georgia was in the south holding out against slavery. Here's a kicker, there were more slaves in New York than any other place in America including southern states at one time or another. I think it's time for the northern states to face their sins against humanity as well. Repent America and pay for slavery. It's too much of a burden to keep carrying around. Come to Jesus and free yourself. One could easily say that New York was the place in the north helping give birth to slavery. Donald Trump grew up in the state of New York, therefore signifying New York as one of the most racist places in the world. However, looking at New York today. It's sweet as can be.

Here's our song "I Could Never Love Another- The Temptations- 1968"

Before I go any further. I have two questions. Is the white race really special and above ever other race? Also, can a white person be a racist if they truly understood that Jesus was a black man? You can rest assured that the answer is NO. Because racist white people think there is some type of divinity in white skin and they have made skin God. Which seems by all accounts would make God prejudice and a racist Well, let me tell you a little bit about white skin. Whites were not recognized on the face of the earth as civilized people until about 300 years ago. So, learn from people. Start with Black Jesus, the truth. I heard white people saying things like. Why should it matter what race Jesus was? Well, it matters because it proves that there is no divinity in being white which is the essence of racism. There were no white people in the Holy land.

Now, there will always be someone who knows the truth. So, keep in mind that we had an American President, Governors, Senators and Representatives. Now, The Civil Rights Leader was neither, yet, he was the true leader. That person is probably sitting back smiling, I know. I believe he will step up, when it's time. Remember we were dealt a hand from the bottom of the deck and it's called cheating. Yeah, and at the same time these people have put a mortgage on the United States of America. They are pirates busy stealing. So, let's straighten out the cards this time. There is nothing to worry about within the Democratic Party. But we need to push harder, and keep an eye on the deck. Whoa, to Donald Trump every day is an adventure in the Twilight Zone and it's not science fiction, but psychological horror. So, let's stay vigilant and continue to hold hands. Stay beautiful people and keep pushing and make sure there is NO backtracking. I love you forever.

Yes, black people are extraordinary people with a strong sense of what is right from wrong. We are making the world what it should be, by creating beautiful colors. I'm so glad we are not tired yet. So, keep rocking and rolling with me and let's finish the job, and always remember Jesus never insinuated violence. If someone is doing that, then they are devil worshippers. Here's our song "Van McCoy - The Hustle and Best Of - The Hustle (Original Mix)

Black people are still chasing the shinning objects. They are afraid to build another black wall street. Therefore, not having a security blanket around their lives leaves them feeling insecure. They should own one of the largest banks in America. But they don't because they are still depending on whites. It appears that blacks with money do not put black business minded people around them. They go straight to whites. Even blacks with money feel the same way as the poor. They are still living in fear. They will only get over the fear when blacks have equality. So, they must push the issues for reparation. It's the balancing act.

White males are brazening and not trying to change, just another macho bully with the best job descriptions.

They are busy trying to find a way to take away black males and white women power, at all cost. It's a philosophy that puts the white women back into the kitchen as a servant and the black man digging ditches. It's a part of their making America great again. Ask the Chiefs kicker. Yeah, it's the same play they keep running and it will not stop. So, brace yourself and hold your ground together. Now, watch it and don't get played again. Because neither one of you are a part of the dominant group and will never be. Unless you work together. It's not in their plans. So, it's time to be the aggressor and take ground, because you're in charge of your vote, so vote together. Now, any vote for a Republican is a flat out vote against yourself and it's thuggish. It's the party that tries to makes everyone look stupid who disagrees with them, they want one mind set. Well, how can they make something great again? When all they have ever done is suppress black men and white women. Their explanation is it's what God wants. NO, God do not punish certain people, because of who they are, because he created everyone equal. Now, they are hiding behind religion calling themselves Christian. But are evil doers that love to follow the devil in the name of Jesus. So free yourself and vote against the play boys club, at the polls. That's your only hope. No more room left for failure, and playing the good little girl, it doesn't work.

I have said time and time again, there are more women than men. So, you win the battle and it should be within your control from now own. Because men will always keep you under attack. Fight back. They say that women are committing murder. But when you look at the scriptures it only says that anyone who hates his brother, have already committed murder. This type of killing needs to stop, before they can point their finger at someone else.

I like to see people trying to better themselves. But, a lot of black rappers are lost within the spider web of the white man and are constantly digging themselves deeper and deeper. They don't seem to understand that the white so call Christians in America hates their music more than anything else. Now, Donald Trump knows that perfectly well. But in order for his con to work, he's portraying to be your friend to lower you into his spider web, only to get black votes. Alright, black rappers have lost touch with reality and have become eccentric people (pointless). Most rappers are so naîve, until they can not see what's coming. First of all, Republicans hate to see you rich, secondly, they hate your popularity and third they hate the nasty talk in your songs. So, it's essential that you grab on to what I'm saying. Because, I'm warning you of the destruction path that's about to take place, if Donald Trump wins the election.

The church will get rid of your music, right away. Rest assure that they will do it, because the church is in charge of the Republic Party these days (but it's impossible to understand their religion). They run things now and your music is unacceptable. So, they are coming after your music first, and it will be easy for them to destroy. Now a part of making America great again is getting rid of your music, for starters. That might leave some of you broke. Because they will make it the law of the land, to take away your music. They don't like their kids listening to that music. So, stop thinking you are so Important, because you are nothing to white Christians, in fact you are at the bottom of the barrel and they will shut you down, if given the opportunity.

If rappers were as smart as they pretend to be in their songs (which is a joke) they would be able to read the preliminary actions beforehand. A word from the wise, this will not be transitory, but prominent. Because your days are limited, if Donald Trump becomes President.

So, you better get out there for Kamala Harris and pray she dominates, because the supreme court is rotten to the core. You have to convey to your followers that Kamala Harris is the best leader. You must become indomitable and resist the con. Yeah, Donald got folks out of jail, which was a good thing. That's over, now let it go. Line up people and keep the line straight, because it's time. It's no longer the strong will survive, but it's in the hands of the ones who truly know how to orchestrate power. Oh, one other thing, if you are a black man that's famous, please get married asap. Because you guys don't know the game, walk away. Here's our song "Harold Melvin & The Blue Notes - Wake up Everybody (Official Audio) ft. Teddy Pendergrass

MOVING ON

The future is shaped by today's decisions. Education and more education are the only answers. One must understand the need at hand.We thought Joe Manchin was normal, but he's not, he has attracted more hate than most people within the Republican Party. He's filled with the white man's fever and it's called structural racism. I'm 100% positive about that. He's a low-class man that's out of control, with his racist ways, which makes him a disgrace to blacks and the entire Democratic Party. He is the Trojan horse. His mission is to destroy the democratic party from the inside because of his hatred toward black people. Oh, by the way, he owns Kyrsten Sinema. He knows she doesn't have all her faculties in place and that she has a two-year-old mentality.

I'd rather have a conversation with any raccoon on the planet than with either one of these pan cakes. Two little love birds. Alright, here's our song "If I Only Had a Brain."

THE END

I can remember the first time I voted. I was 19 years old and it's still one of the most exhilarating things I have ever done. It gave me a sense of direction and I felt like a true adult. It liberated me in a spiritual way unimaginable. Come on, let's work with this thing. I'm going to put this into plain layman terms, just end lunacy. You know how I like plain layman terms, it's a passage that sniffs out wrong like a hound dog. Alright people, we are rolling again. So, let's deal with this scenario, I believe a lot of people can equate themselves with a divorce. Now, as for this day in time blacks have divorced most white people simply because of institutionalized racism that's so unfair and abusive. On the one hand white people are still trying to rekindle this tumultuous abusive relationship with blacks by using verbatim language. Saying just give me one more chance. I'll be a better master this time, aww, unequivocally NO.

Well, the old slave masters may have ruminate right about one thing, like if you learn to read and write BOY, you just might realize I'm fake. All for one and one for all. Please, no more impervious cynical ways of thinking. Alright, show some class. Love your neighbor.

I think one of the hardest things to resonate with a white man is coming to understand that he needs to egress some of his wealth, because he has taken more than his share. In fact, he has my share and have deceived people like me for over 300 years. No one is taking anything from whites. We just want what we deserved and that's equality. Now, I understand that a lot of whites hasn't been in America that long. So, they don't quite understand the situation. But they should keep their mouth shut about America's unfinished business from the past. Because they still get full benefits and it has helped them along. So, stand down. This is something that needs to be addressed by Kamala Harris and her administration. You cannot abuse people like that in the past and simply walk away. America do not leave other races in such bad shape. It has been proven that most black families go back over three hundred years in America. They don't have anything to show for it, because the system shut them out, and it was the law of the land. We need to fix that as soon as possible. Most blacks don't make enough money to buy a house, or nice things for their kids.

It's a shame, because 96% of black people have been here for over 300 years and are still suffering, hungry, Incarceration and homelessness. Along with being harassed and murdered by white police officers. How was America great in the past with all of this stuff going on. It's mind boggling to hear whites say make America great again. I guess it's disrespecting blacks and stealing their wealth. Looks like somewhere along the line whites should recognize the damage they have inflicted upon blacks. Because if you don't see it, then the only thing left is your diagnosis, which is an Intellectual development, which use to be called mental retardation, and that needs to be addressed as soon as possible. Because that kind of thinking makes you a danger to society. There is already enough mental Illness in the world. Do you have to be added on every day of your life? The answer is no. But only you can change that.

Whites have been brain washed into believing all blacks are lazy people who steal and rape. It's all designed to keep white women fearful of black men. They have somehow been effective with that philosophy. So, they keep feeding her fear, so she will never find out the truth. But let me tell you black people are hard workers and believe in doing a good job. Let's start giving each other a fair chance. Not like separate but equal, but together as equal. President Kamala Harris wants to love us all, so let's all love her back. She will truly MAKE AMERICA GREAT by equalizing its people. Well, this train has left the station. Destination, straight to the mountain top. Alright, here's our song "Jackie Wilson - (Your Love Keeps Lifting Me) Higher And Higher (Best Quality).